My Malibu
Death

Amy Weitman

To: Karen
Best wishes,
Juliet

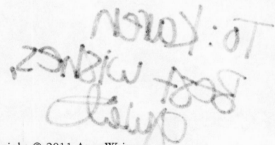

To: Karen
Best wishes!

ISBN: 1456591673
ISBN-13: 9781456591670

One

Deborah wakes to the light from the bathroom. "Shut the door," she says and pulls the white sheet over her head. She closes her eyes and wishes she could disappear. That would count as a talent, she thinks.

She hears the flushing toilet, running water and approaching footsteps. Reluctantly, she peers out from her white tent, her bare face wrinkled from the down pillow.

Dan is standing above her wearing his custom suit. New streaks of grey have invaded his black hair which he wears slicked back with gel. The whites around his eyes are red. His skin is pale. She decides that the pink tie looks nice and grunts at him.

"What's this about?" he asks looking down at her.

"Nothing," she replies.

"I might not make it home tonight," he says, tightening his belt.

"Whatever," she says and pulls the covers over her head. She imagines Dan sleeping on his tan chenille sofa in the downtown office tower, leaving a puddle of drool for his morning client to sit upon.

This is their marriage. Silences filled with anger and disappointment. She hears Dan sigh and walk away. He's out of the room and walking up the staircase. Under her covers, she thinks about her failed attempt to leave him. A year and a half ago she'd began to plan to move, without him, to their Palm Spring's condominium. Despite her lack of a job and without the support of any friends, she was ready to go. That all changed, however, in the dirty bathroom stall at Sav-On Malibu when her urine made two pink lines appear on the strip instead of one.

Now with the sound of the garage door closing she emerges from her temporary hiding place. She leans across the California King bed. She removes her journal and Mont Blanc pen from the nightstand. With her most impressive cursive she writes her suicide note.

March 10, 2007

To whom it may concern:
Please don't be shocked by my death. I have been considering it for some time now. It is no one's fault but my own.

Sincerely,
Deborah Miller

She tears out the lined paper and admires the note for its simplicity. Carefully, she folds it in half and places it back inside the drawer. This will be one of the first places they will look, she thinks, feeling pleased with her abnormal decisiveness.

There are methods of killing yourself in Malibu. Successful movie stars shoot themselves in the privacy of their beachfront estates. Rock stars drive their luxury SUVs off Malibu Canyon. She imagines the cars landing with a fiery thud on the same canyon floor where M.A.S.H was filmed. She remembers the show's opening song was Suicide is Painless. It had been her father, The Captain's, favorite television program.

She thinks about what method would best suit an unemployed, childless housewife.

Two

Deborah wears a pair of designer sweatpants with a mismatched sweatshirt. In the past two years of living here she's learned that the trick of dressing in Malibu is to look as if you haven't really tried. A four hundred dollar sweater paired with flip-flops. Torn designer jeans. Tasseled leather handbags. Valuables disregarded in order to be cool. At least for today she'll appear to fit in.

Not so long ago, assimilation mattered most. Being raised to stay in line translated well into a marriage based on upward mobility: Her college degree hanging on the wall in their office, demonstrating her intelligence despite her unemployment. Buying a weekend home in the desert. Moving into a four million dollar Malibu house and giving up her assistant editing position at Orange County Lifestyle magazine.

At the time, quitting her job made sense. The commute to Newport Beach was too long and soon a baby would be part of their marital plan. Besides, Dan's income and success as the law firm's "youngest-ever" partner significantly outweighed any small achievements that she may have attained along the way: a promotion or two, her photograph in the newspaper at some charity function. She wouldn't get the credit she deserved.

Instead, she's willingly followed the path toward success as carved out by Dan. She knows that she's been a fool to go along like this. But something has changed and her energy is gone. She feels certain that she can't go on living this life. She is tired. Thirty-three years old and already tired.

She walks upstairs. Her footsteps echo off bare walls. She sighs. The kitchen is an array of spotless stainless steel appliances. Though she's still intimidated by its capabilities, she approaches the gourmet coffee maker. She selects a cappuccino. It comes out too hot to hold. She leaves it sitting on the stone slab. Soon Rosa will have the mug washed and put away. Deborah's own sense of order has been lost.

She slides open the door and walks out on the balcony. The wind blows. Palm trees bend toward the choppy grey sea. She looks down at her feet. Her ruby painted toes are numb from the cold stone deck that spans the entire length of the modern 6,000 square foot house.

She's standing above ancient Chumash Indian ground. In the distance she hears the sound of construction, loud hammering and a drill boring holes into the earth. What will remain? The Chumash were also the Sea Shell people; they lived along the California coastline from Malibu to Paso Robles. What would they think, witnessing the Malibu of today: expensive shops, restaurants and homes like her own?

The wind howls. Her face is cold. They're watching me, the Indians, she thinks and considers going back inside. She looks over the iron railing at the ground below. It's a far fall from where she is. If I'm afraid of heights then why am

I living on top of a hill? she wonders. The 180-degree view captivated her when she first walked through the house with Dan and their real estate agent. Deborah looked out of the floor to ceiling glass windows at an endless ocean.

"What do you think?" their agent asked as if he didn't already know they'd be impressed.

"It's perfect," said Dan.

Who says no to the Malibu Dream House? Certainly not Barbie and Ken.

Overcome with the view of the horizon, Deborah never looked down from the balcony to see how far she might fall. Before dying, she'd like to overcome this fear. She tries to remember the mantra given by her hypnotherapist, who claimed to be able to cure her altophobic tendencies. Obviously she has wasted six hundred dollars. A hawk circles her property hunting for prey.

The original owners of the house had been delayed three years trying to wrest the necessary building permits from the City of Malibu Planning and Coastal Commission. Because of the slope, the home took an additional two and a half years to finish. A third of the construction budget was invested in a foundation constructed of caissons drilled one hundred feet deep until they reached bedrock. Sand wasn't strong enough to support the house.

Once it was complete the owners were broke and divorcing. The house was priced to sell.

"We'll take it," said Dan.

Their agent, a well-dressed, sexually ambiguous man holding a Blackberry filled with celebrity clients, seemed pleased. He flashed his best smile. "I'll have my assistant send you the paperwork."

And that was how they bought their home.

Dan said they got a good deal. Maybe she'd felt that way too. She just can't remember anymore. She assumed that her friends in Orange County weren't too far away. She was wrong.

Now, she walks inside and closes the clad doors behind her. A smart design choice, Dan said when they moved in. Wooden doors will rot from the salt air. She hadn't known then that she would rot too.

She runs her fingers through her hair and they get caught in the mess of black tangles. She has a hair appointment, booked two months in advance; it would be rude to cancel at the last minute. Her hairdresser would lose an hour's pay. No one else should be punished for her mistakes. Her father, The Captain, raised her to obey. The suicide will have to wait.

She grabs her handbag from the kitchen table as the phone starts to ring. Wrong number, she thinks. The Captain is dead and her mother left when she was nine. Her in-laws, she suspects, have never liked her much and friends from the past no longer call. She is alone. Except for the first few years of marriage and the time in Orange County with her friends, it's always been like this. A childhood depression that she thought moving out west would cure has returned. Now it sits upon her like a weight just as it had when her mother left. Except this time, it has doubled in size.

The phone stops ringing.

She walks into the garage. Her car is parked inside. The lack of connection with friends may be mutual. They never call her but she never calls them. She acknowledges her laziness and feels a wave of regret.

Things used to be different. When Dan was in law school they lived together in an apartment in Westwood.

She'd finished school and worked part time to assemble UCLA's course catalogues. It had been fun. She and Dan went to local bars and watched sports. They laughed at the same jokes and enjoyed the same food.

Dan graduated, passed the bar exam and their carefree life changed. Late night movies went unwatched. He was too tired. Breakfast dates were hurried. He was too rushed. There was their expected engagement and his multiple job offers. Everything happened simultaneously and so it was often hard to distinguish what event they were actually celebrating. Was it a sparkly new wedding ring or an impressive 401k?

She quit her job in Westwood and he accepted one. They moved to Orange County and rented a small house. Aside from the beach, Orange County reminded her of the Midwest. Everything and everyone living there looked identical-tract homes and plain faces. She knew what to expect in Orange County.

She was hired by the local magazine as a lowly intern and then rose to the position of an assistant editor. Dan worked long hours from the very start. She took a few evening photography classes and made some new friends. They often came over to visit, sat outside on plastic patio chairs and drank white wine from a box. When Dan was home he'd barbecue. She might have been happy then. Seven years went by fast. Her work at the magazine forced her to socialize more than she may have wanted otherwise. She attended local events: restaurant openings, community plays and fundraising galas. If Dan wasn't available, she'd bring a friend. She was determined to make herself happy.

Their rental house was ten blocks from the beach, but they wanted to see the ocean. When Dan was promoted they moved. She thought she'd photograph the sun setting over the water in Malibu. However, she never took out the camera.

She also lost touch with her friends. Neglected friendships faded. It might have been all her fault. A few months after the move they threw a dinner party. Deborah worked with a caterer and carefully selected each of the four courses. She slipped barefoot into a new silk dress and cashmere cardigan. When the doorbell rang her closest friend from Orange County, Heather Mills, and her husband Scott, were the first to arrive. Deborah greeted her with a hug. Dan mixed drinks.

"You never told me the house was this nice," Heather said, eyeing the large empty living room.

"We sold all of our furniture. Shabby chic doesn't look right here," Deborah said even though Heather's home was furnished that way. She'd didn't think about how it might have sounded. She'd only wanted to explain why there was nowhere to sit, not to sound like a snob.

"We're going to eat outside. I had rentals brought in for the deck," Dan said from behind the bar.

"You've outdone yourself this time," Scott said, lifting his martini glass and loudly clinking it against Dan's.

"Show Heather the view from outside," Dan said to Deborah.

Deborah nodded and gestured for Heather to follow. Scott stayed near the alcohol. Deborah walked her friend past the kitchen where a team of chefs prepared dinner for ten. Deborah opened the balcony doors and they stepped outside. The sun had set and the wind blew cold. Heather stood shivering in a light cotton sundress.

"Let me get you a sweater," Deborah said. "It's always cold here. I'm so glad you finally came." She led her friend past the caterers and downstairs into her bedroom. The only furnishings were their king mattress on the floor covered in a white bedspread and two side tables.

"This place is amazing," Heather said.

"It's annoying not to have furniture," Deborah said. Heather shrugged.

"Dan wants to buy things slowly. But it's hard not to have a place to sit during the day," Deborah said.

Heather seemed to ignore her as they walked into the closet. "This is the size of my entire bedroom," Heather said.

Deborah handed Heather a sweater. "I miss seeing you all the time like before," Deborah said. "And Dan's hardly ever here." She wanted to share her loneliness.

Heather was too busy admiring Deborah's built-in handbag cabinet. "This house is beautiful. I'm happy for you," Heather said.

"Still, I miss things the way they were," Deborah said. "And, I haven't taken one photo since we moved." The doorbell rang. Deborah turned and walked upstairs to see who'd arrived. Heather followed and said, "You're so lucky."

After the party Deborah sat in a rental chair on the deck. "I wish they lived closer," she said.

Dan leaned against the balcony and sipped his martini. "You'll meet people," he said.

"I don't know," she said. She listened to waves crash on the beach. "I wonder if we've…"

Dan yawned. "We have quite a view," he said and looked out to the ocean.

It was dark outside. She couldn't see anything.

"I'm going to bed," he said and walked into the house.

There were things that she wanted to say but she didn't want to sound ungrateful. They'd just thrown an elaborate celebration.

By November her discontent had grown. Maybe her isolation in this beach town was thought to be alluring and glamorous. Dinner party invitations were declined. Old friends had babies and the drive to Malibu was deemed too far. But Dan loved Malibu. Of course he did, he could leave it every day and see colleagues.

She secretly plotted to move. In doing so she learned that she was capable of hiding anything from Dan.

Anything except his child.

So when she revealed her pregnancy one night over dinner and he spun her around in his arms and told her he thought she'd seemed hormonal lately, she believed him. She began to doubt her plan. Maybe it was the hormones that made her want to leave.

At that time she was three months pregnant. The fact that she didn't suspect it earlier made her feel inept at motherhood already. Her swollen breasts and waves of nausea should've caught her attention, but she'd been so consumed with her own desires that she'd missed the obvious. When she missed her last two periods, she blamed it on stress and weight loss. Even as she was preparing to end their marriage, their baby was growing inside of her. What kind of maternal instincts did she possess?

Her pregnancy compelled her to stay with Dan. The money she'd stashed away went towards buying maternity clothes and furnishing the nursery. Some days she felt hopeful about creating a family. Other days she cursed the idea of being stuck with her husband forever. Her belly had grown and her feet swelled every afternoon but Dan remained exactly the same. Except, he developed a swaggering "I'm a father" walk that irritated her.

Five months later she miscarried and believed that she'd got what she'd deserved. She knew it when she saw the blood. Her lack of gratitude and her indecision had cursed the baby from the start. Along with the loss of her child also went the little self-confidence that she had left. She had trouble focusing and couldn't finish a book, (not even the Da Vinci Code. Or especially not that.) It was hard to get out of bed in the morning. As for Dan, nothing seemed to slow him down. In fact, last year he made more money than ever before.

Now, Deborah digs inside her purse for the car keys. Instead she finds her cell phone. There are people she could call about her sadness. Mostly they're wives of partners that Dan has introduced her to who live in similar sized houses with staff. But they're still only acquaintances. And over the past two years she's learned that they pay to avoid what they consider life's unpleasantness: A neighbor with a foreign sounding last name is unpleasant. A man begging on the side of the road is unpleasant. A dead baby is certainly most unpleasant, she thinks. She finds her keys and gets into her car. She and Dan had to tell their acquaintances, to cancel the baby shower after the invitations had been printed. She felt that her miscarriage had inconvenienced everyone.

After that she had stopped trying to meet new people. No more would she go out of her way to attend a luncheon with a wife Dan had deemed important. The truth was, it took all her energy to get out of bed each day and make it appear like she was living any kind of a life.

The garage door is closed. She starts the Range Rover but rests her forehead on the steering wheel. It would be difficult to drag out the hose and pass it through the window. Besides, she doesn't want to traumatize Rosa.

Deborah picks her head up, presses a button and opens the garage door. She backs the car out. At the end of her driveway she stops and tries to admire the exterior of her house. It looks to her like a ship, a modern wreck, grey and angular. Tourists have stopped to take pictures. She can't understand why. Trapped on a sinking ship, she thinks.

She opens the car's center console. Inside is Dan's gun.

Three

The canyon walls are collapsing. Deborah is driving to her hairdresser. County workers in orange vests secure plastic sheeting on the sliding hillside. If she makes it out, she'll reach Pacific Coast Highway in ten minutes. The roadside construction, confirms that Malibu is a fragile environment. Years of fires and floods have made this an unstable place to live. She doesn't want to be here anymore.

She reaches PCH and rolls down the windows. She drives past the pier. Malibu smells of dead fish.

At her going away party, in Orange County, an old friend gave her a book, Malibu: A Century of Coastal Living. It said a woman named Rhoda May Rindge inherited Malibu in 1917, but in 1920 the state of California informed her that they'd build a highway through her property. Rindge began a lengthy legal and physical battle, which included horse riders carrying shotguns. In 1926, the state of California opened the Roosevelt Highway. This is the highway she's now on.

Rhoda May Rindge lost, Deborah reminds herself. She drives PCH north past the Malibu Country Mart. There is construction here too. The local lumberyard and hardware store will be reconfigured as luxury- shopping destinations.

Deborah can hardly wait for her hair to be washed with warm water and sweet smelling shampoo by Barbara's assistant. At least her hair will look nice when they find her body.

When sirens approach from behind, she pulls to the side. First, a fire truck and then a swarm of cyclists in fluorescent yellow spandex fly past. What allows them to feel secure riding unarmed along PCH? "Idiots," her father would have said. She too thinks they're crazy. The road clears and she quickly accelerates to fifty-five. If she exceeds sixty, she'll be pulled over by one of the local sheriffs. She sits up straight, remembering that her Pilates teacher advocates good posture.

Deborah reaches the rundown shopping center. As she pulls into the crowded parking lot she finds herself in the daily mix of migrant day workers, anorexic housewives and semiprofessionals fighting as equals for the rare parking spot. After circling a few times, she finds a spot between new silver Mercedes and an old gray Toyota Tercel. This is the real landscape of Malibu.

Deborah turns off the car, gets out and locks the doors. She worries that someone might steal the gun. Her father had always kept his locked up but Dan wanted it to be accessible. He worried about protecting the house and kept it in his underwear drawer. Initially, the gun scared her. She wonders now about her father's reasons for owning one.

"I never thought I'd have to live with one again," she had said when Dan brought it home to Malibu.

"I never thought a lot of things," Dan replied while looking at something else, a pile of bills or the last number dialed on his cell phone.

She gets out of the car and carefully avoids the puddles of septic waste accumulating in the parking lot. Once upon a time she thought she would savor the celebrity excrement, but now she hates the smell of Malibu. It literally makes her sick.

She's late. Against the advice of her facialist, she furrows her brow.

In the salon an older woman is seated in Barbara's chair.

"I'm running behind," Barbara says. "A celebrity client called for an emergency appointment for a last minute photo shoot. You know how those things can be," Barbara says, folding foils into her client's hair.

"I'll wait," Deborah says with a false smile. Her upbringing makes her prescreen any unsavory words she might say. The Captain would wash her mouth with Zest soap when she talked back. Which wasn't often. It didn't take long for her to learn. Certain subjects were taboo: sexuality, fantasy, and the night that her mother left them. Emotions weren't discussed. Deborah's childhood was a routine of school, homework and sleep. The Captain worked, did household chores, and drank himself to sleep. There was no room for emotion.

She crosses her hands in her lap and sits up straight in the uncomfortable wicker chair. It's a posture that she has been groomed for.

She picks up the magazine with a picture of Angelina Jolie and Brad Pitt on the cover. They'd left Malibu to have their child delivered in Africa. Deborah thinks that she herself would have traveled anywhere in the world to give birth to a living, breathing baby.

Three hours and four hundred and seventy five dollars later, Deborah emerges from the hairdresser's with a head of perfectly shiny black hair falling smoothly past her shoulders.

She drives back towards the Country Mart, passing a group of young women running toward Pepperdine University. The church bells from the school are ringing, summoning their virginal bodies towards the white cross at the top of the hill. Ultimately, she knows time will catch up to each of them, even if they continue to run. Inevitably their hair will soon be despoiled with expensive chemicals and their breasts pumped full of saline. This is the natural order of evolution for a woman living in Malibu.

She parks her car she watches the paparazzi scurry about like pigeons. She catches a glimpse of herself in the rearview mirror. Maybe they'll mistake me for a movie star and take my picture, she thinks, and wants to laugh. She runs her fingers through her hair. She opens the car door and feels chilled from the cold ocean air. No one notices her.

Malibu can make a beauty queen feel ugly.

At the Country Mart she waits in line and pays five dollars for a cup of coffee. She clutches it eagerly with cold hands and walks towards the park. Her sweatshirt has been worn thin. The wind blows and it goes right through.

In the distance, she can see tightly bundled children being pushed on the swings by their nannies. Designer strollers are arranged in a line. The park is a rectangular sandbox that local cats use as a litter box.

Deborah stops walking. A tightness seizes her throat, as though someone is trying to strangle her. She sighs, trying to release its grip but it doesn't go away. She takes a sip of coffee. The sweetness from the mocha fills her mouth with so much pleasure that she's able to breathe again. She's convinced that chocolate is better than anything else, even sex.

She throws her cup into the trashcan. She'll go home and walk up the canyon's trail. But she will not return.

Four

Her hands are shaking as she laces her walking shoes. From the back of the closet, next to her camera, she grabs Dan's black canvas backpack. Before they moved to Malibu Dan said, "it's for the weekend hiking we'll do." He read about local trails. But after they left Orange County, weekends became time to catch up on his work and she'd remind herself to appreciate the security his job provided.

She'd left her position at the magazine. She's still amazed at how quickly she was able to walk away from a career that took her six years to build. They'd thrown her a going away party. She'd smiled and pretended to be happy as she ate the cake. Dan was there. She would leave it behind for him. When the celebration was over he thanked her coworkers for organizing it. Children were the next part of the plan.

Deborah rips the plastic tag from the backpack with her teeth and throws it on the floor. Carrying the pack, she walks upstairs and goes into the garage and grabs the cold metal gun from the Range Rover's center console. Before

Rosa can see her, she places it in the open backpack and zips it shut. She slams the car door.

Outside the day is grey. The stubborn marine layer refuses to budge, but the fog makes it a good day for this, she thinks. She imagines that despite her note, Dan will still perceive this as his fault. She tells herself that she doesn't care. Let him feel bad.

It's cold. She could go back inside to get a jacket, but what would be the point? She thinks of Rhoda May Rindge fighting the state in 1920 with her gun drawn, ready to fire at trespassers and highway construction workers. She's inspired but also realizes there's no one here to fight. The streets are lifeless. These homes cost the occupants their freedom. Dan is no exception. Had she pushed him to this life?

She begins her walk and climbs the hill. Soon she descends. Like a snake, the road slowly winds around and through the neighborhood. She knows when she reaches the midpoint of the canyon she'll reach the hiking trail. From there she'll find a secluded spot.

There's no changing Dan, she assures herself. From their days together at UCLA until now, she suspects, he has known exactly what he's wanted.

"I'll take you to eat at Chin Chin," he'd said after a study session. It was his way of asking her out.

She nodded, her long black bangs falling into her eyes. Her depression made her feel invisible even then.

When they first met she was sitting alone, eating an apple and studying in the cafeteria.

"I took that course," he said and pointed to her textbook.

She finished chewing and smiled. "It's tough," she said to the handsome stranger.

"I can help you," he said.

Soon he began tutoring her in public policy. Her depression seemed to lift. If ever he noticed that she was sad he never mentioned it. She suspects that initially he found it attractive. It led to her sense of complacency. She'd go along with whatever he'd plan: watching baseball games, going sailing and bowling. The sorts of things that she found boring but never complained about. In the meantime, he showered her with attention. On dates he'd show up with flowers. After classes he'd be waiting for her. She'd felt flattered.

"She wouldn't have graduated without me," he told acquaintances over the years in recounting the way they met.

She'd laugh along playfully while quietly wondering if he was right.

But, Deborah sees where she's headed. She's lost him over the past ten years. Year by year he slowly gave more of himself to the firm. Once she lost the baby, she found that there was nothing left. She's surprised that she's held on this long.

Maybe if she'd known her mother she could blame this suicide plan on her. Maybe it's faulty genetics, she thinks. Instead, Deborah will blame it on herself.

She notices that her jaw is clenched. She tells herself to relax and tries to study the various landscape designs of her mysterious neighbors. To her left, on the view side, there's another ultramodern estate. Next to that is a Spanish house designed by a local architect. These neighbors are friendly enough to wave from time to time, but the wife is a soap opera star who deeply values her privacy. That seems ridiculous, Deborah thinks, she then thinks of her own melodrama: the suicide note, the gun, herself as a victim. Her face flushes.

She walks slow and looks at the Cape Cod style home painted light blue, with large white-framed windows. When it went on the market a few years ago, the neighbors never imagined it would be purchased by a group that intended to turn it into a Sober Living Center and Rehab. After the sale, the locals banded together to fight the city for allowing the sale. It was the first time many of the neighbors had ever met. "How many recovery centers does one city need," was their argument. There were already well over 30 rehabs in a town with 14,000 residents. Regardless, Malibu granted the permit. The city knew that within in a few months the neighbors would again be utterly engrossed in their lives and the neighborhood would once again become their last priority. When the center had emerged victorious, as predicted, the neighbors made their silent retreat into their multimillion-dollar homes and the comfortable habit of politely ignoring each other.

There's a rustling in the brush alongside the road. Probably a squirrel, she tells herself. What does she have to fear anyway? She's carrying the gun. What am I doing, she wonders.

A door slams and a man walks out of the Sober Living Center. She can see his outline through the fog. He's well built, she thinks and surprises herself. He's wearing a T-shirt and sweatpants with a sweatshirt tied around his waist. As he gets closer she thinks again of the gun in her backpack. Without warning, jagged stomach pains stab her from the inside. She tastes bile in the back of her throat and she knows she's going to be sick. There's nothing to throw up and yet she can't stop it. Before she can take another step, the vomit fills her mouth and she bends over and spews mocha colored liquid onto the dirt-covered road. She leans over with bent knees. She's gagging, inhaling the scent of the liquid in a puddle at her feet. A few brown chunks have landed on her new white walking shoes. Bile fills her nostrils and she begins to dry heave.

The man places his hand on her shoulder and steadies her. His touch instantly warms her. "Let me take that," he says, as he slides the backpack down her narrow shoulders.

What if he finds the gun?

"No," she says standing quickly. Now she feels in charge. She wipes the sides of her mouth with the back of her hand. She looks up into his eyes. They're bright blue. Thin sharp lines reveal that he might be close to forty but everything else about him appears much younger.

"I can get you a jacket," he says, casually brushing the blond hair from his face.

"I'm fine," she says and looks down. He seems calm, as if this kind of thing is normal.

They tell each other their names as they walk around her puddle and she glances at him from the side. He has an interesting profile. A strong jaw-line and a nose that looks like it's been broken more than once.

Although she's been secretly searching the hillside for companionship for the past nine months, she hadn't expected to find it by throwing up in front of the rehab center.

"So you like it here?" she asks, not knowing what else to say. She wipes her mouth again to be sure she's removed all traces of vomit. She feels like a fool.

"I like the water. I'm a scuba instructor," Joe says.

She believes him. He looks like he's spent too much time in the sun.

Their footsteps fall into a rhythm as they pass the mid-point of the canyon. She glances towards the hiking trail. She has the momentum to finish the walk now. She wants to laugh. She's walking with a drug-addicted scuba diver named Joe. He could have been anyone.

"I'm leaving here soon," Joe says. "I have options."

"Those are good things to have," she says. She wishes that she wasn't wearing the backpack. The fog makes it difficult to see the ocean. She walks ahead of him.

"Where I'm going, what I'm going to do, never mind," Joe says. "Truth is my sister's picking me up in her mini van." He catches up with her. "I've been in group therapy," he says. He says he worries he'll wind up like one of those people in Starbucks who'll never pass up the opportunity to tell you how they really are.

"And what do you do? Isn't that the standard question in your circle?" Joe says.

"I've fallen out. I'm in the triangle now," Deborah replies and shrugs. She doesn't seem to fit in anywhere anymore.

"Welcome," he says revealing a smile of nearly perfect teeth.

They reach the bottom of the hill. Deborah enjoys the noise from the traffic on the Coast Highway. Cars race past. She feels exhilarated.

In unison they turn and face the winding road back up. Like a punishment, the wind has started blowing. She knows that the climb will be difficult.

"Are you feeling better?" he asks.

She nods, wishing they could forget the vomiting. Her legs feel strong underneath her small frame as she begins the hike.

"Slow down," he says struggling to catch his breath. His athletic body must have developed naturally, she thinks. She'd worked so hard to shed the twenty-five pounds she gained during her unsuccessful pregnancy, but eventually she lost it, plus five extra, leaving her looking waif-like but strong. The plan to have a child was never thoroughly discussed. It, like everything else, became an assumption. She'd quit her job, settle into the spacious house and have children. Her whole life had led her to this point. There was no plotting the child's conception with a Chinese Lunar calendar. No consideration of sexual positions or herbal supplements to aid fertility. As with everything else, she felt like she had simply fallen into pregnancy. Dan was horny and she was half asleep. Besides, she was over thirty. It was time.

She stops on a small dirt plateau overlooking the ocean. Low clouds drift across the sky. The fog lifts. The sea is a greenish blue. Joe stands beside her and removes a pack of Marlboro Reds and a lighter from his sweatpants pocket. She watches him struggling to light his cigarette in the wind.

"Help?" he asks and extends his cigarette towards her.

Deborah makes a small cup with her hands. Her cuticles are ragged and her nails bitten down. Joe puts the shielded flame to the end of the cigarette and it lights instantly.

"We're a good team," he says, inhaling and letting out a long, dramatic exhale.

She nods. The smell of smoke reminds her of getting sick.

"Beautiful view," he says and looks at her. She smiles. His lips are thin and dry, a mouth not at all like Dan's. Deborah shifts awkwardly. She feels naked. Her face is bare. For moment she pretends that he considers her beautiful. She thinks about kissing him. His chapped mouth on hers. His breath will taste like smoke. So different from Dan, who smells like breath mints and aftershave. It's been a long time since she's been kissed.

She avoids looking at Joe and stares at the water. Something flashes and lifts up from a crashing wave. The bird soars alone up and then across the sky.

"You see that?" she asks, pointing towards the horizon.

Joe follows her long slender finger with his eyes. "What," he says.

It's gone.

"Some kind of bird," she says, squinting.

"Probably a pelican," he replies.

"No," she says.

He takes another deep inhale.

"I have to get home," she says and begins to walk away. She's feeling better. The nausea is gone. She thinks she just needs rest.

"Deb, come by tomorrow," Joe calls from behind.

She turns to him. She likes that he called her Deb. Instantly she thinks that it has transformed her into a whole new person. Options, she thinks. "Tomorrow," she calls back to him.

He smiles and a trail of smoke goes from his mouth into the sky.

She makes her way home without contemplating stopping. A patch of sunlight is fighting its way through the clouds.

Deb walks up the large entryway and in the front door. Quickly, she descends into her bedroom and takes her backpack off and puts it in the rear of her closet. She thinks of the bird, it wasn't a pelican. She opens Dan's top dresser drawer. Carefully lifting his neatly folded underwear, she places the gun inside.

Standing before the full-length mirror, she removes all of her clothing. She admires herself as she thinks of Joe's large hands touching her. Then she crawls into her bed and falls asleep.

Five

She sleeps. Her body twitches. Maybe the soul is fighting for its way back, but the dream is not yet complete. She's an adult wearing a fluffy pink dress made for a three-year-old. The Captain is alone playing solitaire in the dining room.

Deborah's body jolts and she falls to the floor, landing with a soft thud onto the Berber carpet. She lays there startled that she's relieved to be awake.

It's daybreak. A light spreads out across the horizon. Traffic explodes onto Pacific Coast Highway. Dan is working in his downtown high rise. Rosa is walking the streets of South Central to catch the Metro bound for Malibu. And Deborah is alive on her bedroom floor. A new day is set into motion.

But something has changed. She pulls herself off of the floor. She can see a school of dolphins in the ocean below. She remembers the dolphins swimming alongside the sailboat in Catalina. On their second date Dan had taken her sailing. He navigated the boat shirtless, through the crystal clear waters. His smooth, tanned muscles flexed under the hot sun. Deborah leaned over the edge of the boat and vomited into the ocean. The dolphins followed along beside them.

She thought then that it had been seasickness. Now she wonders if it was just a sign of things to come in a future with Dan. Had she ever been happy with him? She can't recall.

The relationship started off with a sense of excitement. She'd finished work early one Wednesday and he picked her up from campus. Instead of driving back to their apartment to watch a movie and order in Chinese food, he suggested a drive up the coast. It was a warm summer evening and she'd agreed.

Dan had graduated from law school the past weekend. His parents had flown home, and he'd seemed relieved. Then it seemed like summer would be a continual celebration. Deborah felt free. She rolled down the car windows and he drove them out of the city. Even though she suspected he'd propose on this particular outing, once he parked the car, her heart pounded. They got out and walked barefoot along the beach. He held her sweaty hand and got down on bended knee. He told her that he loved her and presented a two-carat diamond ring. She attempted to say "yes," but he stopped her before she could answer. He pulled out a piece of yellow lined paper from his pocket and read a list of what she'd have to agree to as his wife. She smiled as he read and thought it was his nerves speaking:

1. They must be financially stable before ever discussing the possibility of children. One boy and one girl, but no pets ever. He hated cats and dog hair on furniture.
2. That she remain a nonsmoker.
3. That she remain loyal and faithful to him at all times.

She laughed when he finished, called him silly, and with a quick kiss said "yes."

Now she realizes that the joke was on her.

Six

Deborah's engulfed by the steady stream of shower water pouring from all directions. She pictures a sunny day at the beach. She'll buy a new black bikini and learn how to surf. Gidget, she thinks and smiles. Malibu teenagers will skip school and sunbathe topless in private coves.

She towels herself off and pulls on a clean pair of sweats and a hundred dollar T-shirt with hopeful words silk screened across the back. Love, Freedom, Peace.

Carefully, she applies her makeup in her magnifying mirror, her enlarged pores 10x their normal appearance. Suddenly, she wonders what her mother looked like at this age. Thirty-three. Deborah was eight. The next year her mother left them.

Deborah woke up one sun filled morning and her mother was gone. All of her belongings had been packed into two suitcases. Her father's eyes still red from crying. If there was a note then what did it say? If the Captain were alive, would she have the nerve to ask?

She turns from the mirror and gazes outside. Clouds move across the sky. She remembers having found an old hairbrush matted with long black curls and lipstick-stained cigarette butts under the rosebush. All other evidence of her mother's existence was destroyed. The house became quiet.

Memories of her mother are hard to conjure. Deborah wonders if in an attempt to protect herself, she's blocked them from her mind. She turns back to the mirror. Her makeup looks good. She doubts that she's that powerful to block them.

Deborah's hungry. Her industrial sized refrigerator is empty except for a gallon of expired milk and a rotten head of lettuce. She hasn't eaten since yesterday afternoon. She drives to Ralph's market.

Her father died a few years after her wedding, sudden heart failure. She knew it would happen without warning, that he too would go without saying goodbye. In college she read the newspaper and listened for reports of commercial airline crashes. He was a pilot. At least he would have been doing something that he enjoyed. Flying was the only time that she imagined him happy.

Inside the store, she spins her shopping cart around the wide aisles like a dance partner. In the deli section she selects a pre packaged Chinese chicken salad. In the produce section she watches a young blond woman slowly inspecting an apple in a carefully manicured hand. She admires the woman's attention to detail. She's not like the other Malibu women who quickly throw their organic fruit into plastic bags. Deborah smiles as she passes the blond. Maybe they could be friends. Despite the clanking of Deborah's cart the blond gazes right past her. It's as if she doesn't really exist. She feels like a ghost.

At the checkout line, the blond's items are neatly bagged. Deborah realizes they never could have been friends anyway. The woman's bags are loaded with diapers, wipes, whole wheat breads, no sugar added peanut butter, green organic vegetables, fresh meats and ripe fruits. She shops like a mom.

Deborah leaves the store and digs through her groceries, desperately looking for her salad and accompanying plastic fork. She finds it and begins to eat right in the lot. She's been starving.

Seven

Something very large, like a body, jumps out of the bushes and onto the canyon road. Deborah slams on the brakes. She stops. She's avoided hitting whatever or whoever it was. She takes off her seat belt and looks back to check. A figure rises up from the pavement. It's a girl. She's braless and wears a dirty white tank top. Her breasts are small and her straw colored hair is long and matted.

Deborah stares, she cannot drive away. The girl is standing in the middle of the road and crying.

Deborah gets out of the car. "Are you okay?" she asks. A dumb question.

The girl shakes her head. She points to her arm, which is bleeding. Deborah walks towards her. The girl says, "Help me."

"Come with me" says Deborah, although somewhat reluctantly. Deborah walks back towards the car and hears a sound behind her. The girl has collapsed. Deborah rushes back, reaches around the girl's waist and struggles to pull her over to the car. The girl is unconscious. Half dragging and half carrying, Deborah moves toward the passenger door and hoists her up, pushes her onto the backseat. She slams the door and dashes to the driver's side and speeds back down the hill.

The girl has regained consciousness, she's crying. Deborah is filled with anxiety. "No doctors," the girl says. "I won't go."

"I understand," says Deborah. She realizes now that she still blames them.

The girl stops crying.

Deborah drives to the bottom of the canyon. She stops and looks both ways before turning onto PCH. Maybe she'll drive to Urgent Care anyway. She sees the road is clear but also notices a familiar figure. It's Joe. He's smoking a cigarette. Has he gone for a walk without her? She is surprised by her narcissism. With a trembling hand she rolls down the passenger side window and calls his name.

He looks towards her car suspiciously as she frantically waves her arms. He throws his half smoked cigarette to the ground and runs towards the car.

"We need help," Deborah says.

He climbs in. The traffic clears and Deborah realizes that she's heading north with a dying girl and a drug addict.

Eight

Joe says that he should have left rehab weeks ago. Now here he is in another mess just one hour after group therapy. "Turn around and go to Santa Monica," he says.

Deborah keeps driving north over the speed limit. "There's an urgent care up the road."

The girl in the back seat starts to cry. "I'll jump out of the car," she says. Her swollen hand is on the car door handle.

"Keep it together," Joe says, turned around in his seat.

"You promised me. I trusted you," says the girl.

"What's she talking about?" Joe asks.

"You need help," Deborah says, staring straight ahead. She's afraid she'll crash if she takes her eyes off the road.

"What's this about?" asks Joe impatiently.

"She said no doctors," Deborah says. "Maybe it's a religious thing." She remembers a tiny dress hanging in the closet of her childhood home. Her mother made it for her baptism. If she ever had faith then it's been lost.

"So what?" Joe replies.

The girl pounds on the window with her good hand. "Let me out," she cries. She tries to open the locked door.

"I don't blame her. You can't trust them," Deborah says. The doctors had said that it was a normal pregnancy. Deborah's driving 80 miles an hour.

"How about taking her to a healer?" Joe asks, as if accustomed to not being taken seriously. "I've heard of these women from the center. Our yoga teacher said they have some kind of power."

Deborah ignores him. She drives PCH past The Point, an eclectic mix of humble ranch houses and estate properties. Johnny Carson's former home had been listed for sale at 65 million dollars that month.

"She's passed out," Joe says glancing in the backseat.

Deborah looks back. "Shit."

She accelerates. Her heart is pounding. She turns left off of PCH and pulls into the parking lot of Malibu Urgent Care. It's a rundown single story building. She park and runs inside, leaving Joe alone with the girl.

"Help!" she says to the woman at the desk, who looks at her calmly and continues to chomp on her gum.

"Sign in. You'll have to wait your turn just like everyone else," the receptionist says, rolling her eyes.

Deb turns to find a line of a dozen or so permanently stunned women waiting to sign up for the day's Botox clinic.

"I don't care about lines," she says. "A woman is dying." Her own bluntness comes as a surprise.

The double glass doors slide open and Joe walks in carrying the limp girl.

The receptionist gasps and stands up from her chair. "Dr. Scotty! Come quick," she calls.

Deb wonders if they have made a mistake bringing her here. Maybe she would have been better off going to the healer.

Nine

Deborah finds herself joining Joe in a mock prayer position on the cold metal seat. Her elbows on her knees, her hands clasped and her head dropped. She looks at the floor. Joe places his hand on her kneecap. She lets it sit there as the warmth of his palm magically travels up her thigh. He looks at her and their eyes meet. "Some morning," he says.

She fakes a smile. Can he tell? she wonders.

"I've been to lots of these places. They're all the same," he says.

Deborah nods and pretends that she understands.

"One of my buddies overdosed last year," he says.

"I'm sorry," she says. Is that a stupid thing to say?

"You'd think that I'd have slowed down the partying after that. But it got worse. I was a mess," he says, standing up. He walks towards the bathroom.

She's shocked by his honesty. She's never heard a man admit his weakness. It's attractive.

She picks up a local magazine, Malibu Today, with advertisements for acting classes, investment opportunities, colonics and massages. She flips through the pages and determines that she exists in a wasteland of expensive self-help. Everyone's searching for something just outside his or her reach.

Even as they were moving to Malibu, Dan suggested that they find a canyon property to fix up and flip for profit.

"Aren't we already stretching ourselves?" she asked. She knelt on the floor next to a packed cardboard box. They were in their almost empty living room in Orange County. She held a tape gun.

"We'll be fine," he said.

She looked up at him and tried to smile. Then she rolled the tape along top of the cardboard box. It made a loud noise. She cut the tape with the gun's metal teeth. The box was sealed.

"Now that you're not working it'd be a good hobby," he said.

An expensive one, she thought. She wasn't interested in fixing houses. She enjoyed her photography classes. Still, the hobby she'd devoted herself to most of all was Dan. She couldn't remember anything else that interested her more than him. Even as his work continued to steal him away from her she still held on tight to the belief that one day he'd slow down enough to return to her. Maybe they'd take the time to watch movies again. They could afford season tickets for UCLA basketball games. She hoped he'd adapt to the slower pace of Malibu life. She'd encourage him to skip work. They could walk on the beach and hold hands like they did when they were first engaged. But after two years of living in Malibu, she's given up hoping that he'll change.

Joe returns. "I've got to smoke," he says. He grabs her hand and pulls her up. "Come outside with me."

She follows Joe like a lost puppy. She notices how ironically strong his drug addicted body looks. His shape is appealing to her. She remembers her first crush. He was the captain of her high school swim team. Tan smooth skin curved over new muscle. That was her first encounter with lust, she realizes now.

Joe leads her towards the exit.

She lived in a typical Midwestern suburb. The town was close enough so that her father could drive to the O'Hare airport for work but far enough away from the city to keep Deborah out of trouble. At least that's what he told her. After her mother left, her protection became his priority.

"I've had enough of this life," her father said one night with a sad drunken stare. It was one of the few thoughts he revealed. Usually he sat and drank quietly at night. "Don't you disappointment me too."

And so she kept her head down and studied hard.

Joe holds the exit door open for her.

She still remembers the swimmer's name was Billy Hamden. At swim competitions he wore a yellow cap. He was six feet tall with wide shoulders and narrow hips. A scar on his stomach revealed that his appendix had been removed. She can remember him better than herself.

She worked at the snack bar during swim meets. She thinks that she wore braces then and had frizzy hair. There are no pictures of her. The photo albums disappeared when her mother left. The camera was put away.

Billy Hamden had never noticed her.

Outside the Urgent Care, Joe savors his cigarette. He makes it look like a comforting habit. They sit on a dirty cement bench. Joe removes his sweat jacket and ties it around his waist. "She wanted to die," he says. Two pigeons are walking near their feet.

"Do you think she's going to?" Deborah asks. Joe seems well accustomed to death. The pigeons inspect the cigarette ash. The memory of her father's death and the events that followed are unclear. She has a hard time recalling that particular time, though she's certain she remembers Dan beside her at the barely-attended funeral.

Joe throws his half-smoked cigarette on the ground. "Come on," he says, standing and putting his arm around her shoulders as they walk back inside. The women look up from their US Weekly magazines.

"How's she doing?" Joe asks the receptionist as he removes his arm from Deb's shoulder. She wishes he hadn't. For the first time in months she hadn't felt alone. She and Dan hardly touched anymore, unless by accident.

"Don't know," Cynthia says, still chewing the gum, and Deborah remembers them: this lazy receptionist and the male nurse. It's been only a year and yet she realizes that until this moment she had forgotten: Dan took her here that afternoon when she began to bleed. She wishes the memory away, but it remains. Blood had dripped down her bare tanned legs. She had been wearing a new summer dress. It reminded her then of her first period, unexpected and frightening, her father was in the next room and she was without any necessary supplies. The miscarriage was like that.

Deborah gasps for air. She realizes that this memory can't just disappear. She'd thought that her only option out of this pain was suicide. But, this can't be true. There has to be another way out.

Joe turns to her. "You all right?"

"No," she says. She doesn't want to die.

A woman in platform shoes teeters over to the receptionist desk, smelling like Chanel No. 5 and apple martinis. Tossing her long blond hair over her faux tan, she attempts to whisper, "I'll miss my son's play if I don't get to see Dr. Scotty first."

Joe leads Deborah back to an empty seat.

The receptionist shakes her head and the blond sits back down as an ambulance arrives. Paramedics stroll in the sliding doors, carrying a stretcher. The ocean breeze fills the waiting room. The receptionist steps out from behind her desk. Deborah remembers that they'd come for her here too. She thinks of her baby's ashes littering the Pacific Ocean. What had she felt then? Was it relief? The memory haunts her.

A baby was an expectation, but in truth, she had never taken care of a baby before. As a teenager she never babysat. Her part time jobs involved pumping cheese on a plate of chips at the snack bar. Filing papers during summers in an empty office. Would she have been able to even care for a baby?

And Dan, would he have helped? She's certain that his job would've entitled him to a sense of laziness regarding the baby. Sure he'd display photographs on his desk. But she's certain he wouldn't have changed a diaper.

A door opens and Deborah watches as the girl is carried on a stretcher. The smell of her body odor fills the air. No one else will look at her.

Dr. Scotty comes out a few minutes later. "She was bit by a rattlesnake," he says to Deborah. They administered an antivenin and gave her an IV with fluids. "The biggest risk right now is that she'll have an allergic reaction to the antivenin. She's in shock, she'll probably have to stay in a hospital for three to four days." He crosses his arms on his chest.

"What's her name?" Deborah asks.

"Maria Vasquez," he replies. "We still need some additional contact information from her."

"Maria Vasquez." Deborah pictures the pale girl with straw colored hair.

"Two areas for the cost of one today," Dr. Scotty says, looking hard at Deborah.

She looks down at the tiled floor. It needs to be washed.

"And who's covering the payment?" the receptionist asks.

"I will," Deborah volunteers. Maybe all her money will be good for something, she thinks. After all, it's all Dan really wanted. Money. She thought back to when they were first married. Certainly, she must have thought that it could be enough for her too, she's just not sure anymore.

Despite the Malibu lifestyle, the designer clothes, car and house, she wants simple things: love, friendship and trust. For the last year she has suffered silently. Her grief comes second to Dan's needs. She wonders if they ever shared these thoughts. Certainly they must've had something meaningful that kept them together for ten years. Her anger clouds memories of any good moments.

Dr. Scotty puffs out his chest and turns to the receptionist to proclaim that the Botox clinic can resume.

Ten

Deborah and Joe drive back down PCH. Deborah signals and turns left. "This is where I found her," she says, pausing at side of the road, where the hiking trail begins. Yesterday, she'd planned to go in that direction. She'd even written a note. Now she's anxious to go home and tear it up. Something has changed.

"She was lucky you stopped," Joe says while gazing towards the brush.

Deborah feels her face grow hot when she looks at him. His hair is light from the sun. He's attractive, not handsome. "Sure, I'd stop. Who wouldn't?" she replies.

He shrugs. "Most people would've kept driving," Joe says.

Deborah looks in her rearview mirror to make sure no cars are behind her. She puts her car into park. "Would you have stopped?" she asks. Again she looks at him. A feeling of desire tickles her insides. His answer is important to her.

She wants to know more about him. Where did he come from? What does he want in life? How does he look when he's sleeping?

"I got in the car, didn't I?" Joe says.

Deborah notices a thin scar on his chin. "You still didn't answer," she says. She notices that she's holding her breath. She runs her fingers across the leather steering wheel.

"Sure," he replies.

Deborah puts the car into drive and continues up the hill. She is embarrassed for feeling this way and hopes it's not obvious. She's too old for a crush. She stops at Horizons. Joe gets out and walks around the front of the car to her window.

"Are you okay now?" he asks.

Deborah meets his eyes. "I'm starting to be," she says. It feels honest. She allows herself that hope.

"I'd like to see you again. Come by tomorrow," says Joe, watching her closely.

Deborah nods. She fixes her eyes on the road ahead of her and drives away.

Eleven

The bird comes to her in a dream. It's dark outside. She stands barefoot on the balcony. I've been here before, she thinks but can't remember when. A flash lights up the ocean, and there it is flying across the sky. Its wings are golden and its crown is red. She wants to catch it but she tumbles over the edge.

She wakes up before she lands. It's hard to say if she would have survived the fall.

It's light outside. She's alone in bed. Dan came in after she fell asleep and left before she awoke. The garage door is closing. She gets up and pulls on a pair of new jeans and a crisp white blouse. She walks upstairs.

Rosa's washing Dan's breakfast dishes.

"Good morning," Deborah says.

"Hello missus," Rosa says.

Instead of her usual retreat back into solitude, Deborah finds herself desperate to share yesterday's strange events. She launches into a frenzied description of her encounter with the girl from the canyon and the snakebite, but after she's done, she realizes that Rosa hasn't understood half of what she's said.

Deborah goes to the kitchen desk and looks though a pile of mail. She needs to look busy to hide her embarrassment.

Yesterday Joe said, "I'd like to see you again." Today will be different. She can visit Joe. She can check on Maria in the hospital, although she doesn't believe that's her real name. There are people to help beside herself. She thumbs through the Saks catalog and throws out the junk mail.

The smell of Clorox burns her nose. Rosa is scrubbing the sink. Would that clean the bloodstains in her car? She remembers the suicide note. She runs downstairs to her bedside table and unfolds the lined paper. She reads the note again and walks into the bathroom. She shakes her head, crumples the note into a ball and throws it in the trashcan.

At once she decides that she'll go to the hospital. She'll see the snakebite girl again.

She checks herself in the mirror, but instead sees a pale thin girl with matted blond hair. It's the girl she rescued. Why does she see "Maria's" face in the reflection instead of her own?

Who have I become? She wonders. Deborah closes her eyes and covers her face with her hands. Stop it, she thinks. She tries to fight the familiar self-pity but can't quit what has become habit.

It could be that she never knew what she needed. When her mother left, life with her father became a boring routine. There was school, homework and sleep. She'd spend hours reading books about girls whose lives she imagined as harder than her own. Poor Anne Frank.

There was no time for emotion in a house run by a captain. Besides, since her mother left, he had become an empty shell.

Deborah's head aches. "Stop it," she says. She takes down her hands and faces her reflection. She sees her own green eyes. Vacant, she thinks. For the first time she sees herself.

Twelve

She pulls into the hospital valet line behind a large white Suburban with a bumper sticker that says Jesus is my Co-pilot. She thinks of her father in his TWA uniform. He could fly state to state and still make it home on time for dinner. He just couldn't talk about the night that her mother left.

Deborah's mouth is dry. So dry that she can almost taste it. She can smell the dried blood in the back seat. She thinks that she's making a mistake. She puts her car in reverse but another car blocks her way. She has no choice but to go forward. The parking lot is full. Reluctantly, she gives her keys to the Mexican valet. She hasn't been to the hospital since her miscarriage. She reminds herself that she is capable of facing this.

She walks in and approaches an eldery woman seated behind a large desk.

"What room is Maria Vasquez in?" Deborah asks.

"332," the woman says and points Deborah in the right direction.

Under the fluorescent lighting the old people already look dead. An old man leans on the arms of a reluctant looking caretaker. A frantic mother quickly pushes a crying baby in a stroller.

Outside the room, Deborah takes a deep breath. The long corridor smells like cafeteria food. She opens the door. Light pours in from a bay window. Deborah's black flats click across the floor. She's freezing. Maria is lying under a large blanket, eyes wide open as she stares at the white wall across from her bed where a small gold Christ hangs on a crucifix. Her blond hair has been washed and brushed back from her face.

"Maria, do you remember me?" asks Deborah.

She nods. "Really my name is Amber," she says. She covers her face with her hands. Deborah can see the small blue veins through her nearly translucent skin.

She walks to the side of Amber's bed. "I'm confused about the name," she admits and sits down on a small uncomfortable chair.

Amber lowers her eyes. "I'm sorry for the trouble."

"Can I help?" Deborah asks, feeling obligated.

Amber shakes her head. "You live too close to the danger."

"What do you mean?" Deborah asks. She sits up straight.

"You should leave now," Amber says.

Deborah stands and begins to back away toward the door, bumping into someone when she reaches the hallway. She turns around to see a familiar looking woman, professionally dressed in a beige pantsuit. Her skin is the color of honey.

The woman lays a large hand on Deborah's small shoulder. Her thick black hair is pulled tightly up from her face.

"What a coincidence. Deborah Miller. It's a small world," the woman says. Deborah can almost place her but not quite.

"It's so good to see you looking so well," says the woman. "Were you the one that found her?"

Deborah nods, afraid to reveal much more.

"Is there anyone here to help her?" Deborah asks, wanting to walk away.

"We're looking for her family. I have your home number, Deborah, in my files," says the woman "I'll call you if anything comes up."

Deborah turns quickly toward the long hallway leading toward the exit. She passes an open door where a woman is crying. Past another open door, a baby begins to scream.

People are dying here.

She reaches the end of the hallway and looks back. The woman is still staring at her. Alice Edwards, she remembers. She haunted by the feeling of cold metal between her legs. A doctor scraping out the remains of her dead baby. Alice Edwards looking down at her. Deborah wants to run. Quickly, Deborah turns a corner, still scared that someone has followed her.

Thirteen

Dan's silver seven series BMW is in the driveway. It blocks her spot in the garage. Deborah shakes her head. She pulls along the curb and parks. She looks at her house. It's a long grey wall. There's coldness here, she thinks. Still, she's relieved to be out of the hospital. Going there had been a mistake, she decides. She turns off the car, grabs her handbag from the passenger seat, opens the door and gets out. The street is empty. She leans back against her car and it warms her. Her feet hurt and she feels like crying but she can't.

How will she explain the recent days to Dan? She imagines he'll worry about entanglement issues with Amber. Maybe he'd be right. Still, the girl needed help. Deborah can't pretend things are normal. Besides, she is tired of make believe.

Will she tell Dan about Joe? Just the thought of Joe makes her blush. When he was next to her she could feel herself breathe again. She decides that it will be best not to mention Joe's role in the rescue. Despite Dan's flaws, he's smart. She would hate for him to notice her interest.

A neighbor she's seen before drives past. She feels invisible here. It's a childhood feeling. There's a lack that's greater than missing old friends and family. It's an emptiness. Has she ever felt a connection? There were moments in Orange County that she thinks she had. Maybe she had grown up a bit while living there. But now, standing in front of her Malibu home, she's sure that she's back to the place she started back in the Midwest. Was this sense of isolation her destiny?

Deborah turns and walks to the front door. For a moment, she imagines finding Dan in their bed with Ashley, his twenty three year old assistant who wants to be a lawyer or an actress. After all, Deborah considers that she might not be alone in her feelings of loneliness.

She opens the door and walks in. She hears Dan's voice. He sits on the kitchen barstool and talks into his Black-Berry. Strangely, she feels disappointed. It would be easier if she had found him with Ashley. Deborah would scream and throw things. It would be justified. From his tan slacks and green collared shirt, she knows he's spent the afternoon golfing.

Dan's deep voice purrs about some business deal into the phone. He's affectionately restating the details – a language of partnerships, acquisitions and mergers lovingly shared. And here she is, his wife, eavesdropping on his affairs. This is her fault. When she married him, she knew the rules. Certain numbers appearing on the cell phone signaled the necessity to halt all other activities no matter what. He had even taken a business call in the emergency room during her miscarriage. Why was it that it felt like only her loss?

If the baby had lived Deborah would have a little girl. Dan would have silver framed photos displayed on his desk. He'd quote information on new parenting fads. There'd be ballet recitals and piano lessons. Deborah stops herself. And what would she have? A child to take care of, and what would that mean? She lost her before she had a chance to hear her cry. In the first months that followed the miscarriage Dan had designer furniture delivered almost daily, to fill their empty house. It arrived at her door like some kind of consolation prize.

"How do you like the new chaise lounge?" Dan asked over the phone from work.

"It's nice," she said.

"And the Turkish rug?" Dan asked.

"Great," she replied.

Now she looks around her fully furnished house. One year after the miscarriage and it's decorated with all the "right pieces." Modern art hangs on the wall: Bold graphic words, geometric shapes, abstract and colorful images. What's the meaning behind the expensive images, she wonders and feels cold.

Dan is still sitting on the kitchen barstool, his back towards her. Deborah clears her throat. Dan turns. He glances her way, barely nods and returns to his conversation. She feels dwarfed in the large entryway. It's like she shouldn't be here at all. Suddenly she wants to leave. The feeling is so strong that she wants to run. Instead she turns around and walks at a normal pace out the front door. Outside, the wind blows. She feels it from behind. It helps push her up the hill and then back down. It blows her to the front door of Horizons. And then it stops.

Fourteen

"Does the smell bother you?"

The greeting stuns her.

"Sage," says the frizzy redheaded woman who's opened the door. She's wearing a purple muumuu and Birkenstocks. "We keep the good energy flowing." She smiles when she introduces herself, revealing a gap between her two front teeth.

Deborah takes the woman's large clean hand, happy for its warmth. "I'm looking for Joe," she says. She walks in the entry and past an antiqued table adorned with white roses. Amber-hued light filters down a long spiral stairway.

"Joe is finishing group," says the woman, who Deborah notices is pregnant. She's a large woman and so the pregnancy looks comfortable on her. Deborah remembers looking like she was carrying a beach ball under her t-shirt. She wonders now if her depression is as apparent as her belly was.

She shifts the weight on her feet and looks around the large house. "I don't want to violate your rules. We helped this girl, and I'd like to tell him how she's doing," Deborah says. After this lame explanation she realizes that she has no idea of Joe's last name. How ironic, she thinks, that this basic information wasn't shared. Yet she couldn't stop herself from coming here.

"He'll be coming downstairs any minute," the woman says as Deborah follows her into a cheerful yellow kitchen.

Pots and pans clank loudly while two Hispanic women set furiously to cooking dinner, totally oblivious of Deborah's presence. The smells of butter, lemon and chicken fill the room.

Chatter and footsteps from the second story: the group is coming down stairs. Seconds later, the kitchen is full of conversation and coffee cups.

Deborah feels steady when she sees Joe from across the room.

Joe smiles warmly.

She walks towards him. Everyone is looking at her. She feels like an outsider crashing a high school party. The patients are all good-looking and well dressed.

"Let's go into the living room, Deb." He leads her away from the prying eyes. She turns to look back as they filter through a pair of French doors to the back patio.

Outside, they're drinking coffee and smoking cigarettes. It looks like a party despite the obvious lack of alcohol. Maybe I should go into rehab, she thinks but then can't think of a single addiction that she has. Except to her depression perhaps.

He leads her through to the entry hall and then onto the front porch. Deborah sits on a wooden rocker that she hadn't noticed earlier, so focused on seeing Joe again that she'd only seen the front door. Joe faces her and leans against the white wooden railing.

"She says her name is Amber," Deborah says.

"Maybe she was shrooming," he says.

Deborah looks past him at the smooth ocean and she rocks back and forth. "They can't find her family. Maybe I'll offer her my guest room," she says and then silently changes her mind.

Joe clears his throat. "That's nice," he says.

The smog from LA fuels a brilliant pink sunset.

Joe lights a cigarette and leans back on the railing. He exhales a long trail of smoke. "I'd like to see you away from here," he says. A look appears in his eyes; it reminds her of Dan and she's startled by it. It must have been from a time when they still desired each other. In the first few years of their marriage they made love almost every day, no matter when he arrived home from work. Late nights Dan would slip into bed and warm himself against her naked body. She was always willing to give herself. As his caseloads increased his want for her became less apparent. A long day's reward became sleep.

Malibu looks iridescent. Deborah keeps rocking and thinks of Dan waiting at home.

"I'm leaving in two days," Joe says, taking in the cigarette as deeply as he can.

The sun has set. His smoke covers her like a veil.

She bites down on the insides of her cheeks. "I need to get home for now," she says and stands and walks past him to the steps. She can feel him watching. She takes each concrete step slowly, enjoying his attention. One by one she descends and then turns back to him.

"See you tomorrow," he says.

She wonders if she can wait that long.

Fifteen

When she walks in Dan is still sitting at the kitchen counter. "Where were you?" he asks looking at her suspiciously.
"I came home early, you were gone and then you left again."

She looks at him and feels repulsed. He'd obviously
moved from the stool to shower and change, his black hair
combed back, a light blue button down shirt tucked into a
pair of designer jeans. Metrosexual tendencies are a turnoff,
she decides. These obsessive grooming habits that lead him
to the shower every time after sex.

"I went for a walk," Deborah says and wipes beads of
sweat from her forehead. Joe is masculine and strong.

"Why don't you clean up," he suggests. "Madison said
she'd save us a table. And wear that blue dress. Unless you
ate with someone else," he says sarcastically.

If only he knew, she thinks. "Sounds great," she replies
while wanting to hurl one of his crystal golf trophies at his
face. "I'll get ready."

She walks downstairs to change and shower off the
smell of Joe's smoke, even though she doesn't want to. I'm
married, she tells herself.

It wasn't the sex that held their marriage together for ten years; it was the knowing that Dan would be there. She remembers the small bathroom they'd shared for seven years in Orange County. Dan's toothbrush next to hers in the medicine cabinet, his work shirts neatly hung in their closet, his favorite coffee mug left out by the sink in the morning. These familiar things let her carry on as his wife.

Now in the privacy of their bathroom she lets her clothes drop onto the cold marble floor. She turns on the shower, steps under the warm water and longs for Joe. She blames the move to Malibu for driving her away from Dan. It was the beginning of the end. There were no loud fights, no throwing things across a room or name-calling. Instead, they'd drifted apart. He had his own sink now, in a bathroom big enough for more than two. Their closet was divided into two separate areas so they didn't have to face each other's personal belongings anymore. Success was ending their marriage.

She turns off the water and dries herself with a towel. Quickly, she pulls on her undergarments and steps into the dress that he selected for her. She puts on a silver bracelet. Despite everything, a small part of her is still willing to try. She slips into her heels and climbs up the stairs. She's not sure how to begin the conversation. She straightens her dress and smoothes down her hair.

"Dan," she says.

"We're late," he says, interrupting her.

She follows him outside and into his car.

They drive to Nobu in silence and park.

Outside, it smells like an overripe septic tank. Inside the restaurant it's jasmine and sake. Under a bamboo roof, they sit in a low-lit room eating hundreds of dollars worth of sushi with other Malibuite couples who all politely ignore one another. Each time the front door opens, everyone, including the sushi chefs, turn their heads in unison to see if it's a celebrity. Disappointedly, they turn their attention back to their food when it's just a regular customer.

Deborah picks at her spicy tuna roll with a chopstick. Her long arms look thin with the large silver bracelet around her petite wrist. She removes the fish from the seaweed and rice roll and feeds herself small bird-like bites. Her eating allows her a distraction from Dan. Besides, he's busy scanning the restaurant for familiar faces.

An elderly gentleman and a young blond even slimmer than Deborah approach the table. Dan finishes chewing and wipes his hands with the linen napkin. He stands and shakes their hands. "What an amazing coincidence," he says. "Jim is the new client I was just telling you about," he tells Deborah. "What a small world."

She has no idea what conversation he's referring to. They haven't spoken since they left the house.

"That's why we live in Malibu. It's the type of town where you get to see everyone you know," Jim says. He speaks in a husky voice that matches his body.

"I was just telling Deborah that we need to schedule a dinner," Dan says. "Deborah and Nancy both share a passion for charity work," he tells Jim as if the wives weren't there.

Deborah nods and holds her lips tightly together.

Jim's wife smiles. The light from her five-carat diamond catches Deborah's eye as Nancy bends her wrist to show it off. "You just have to get involved in Operation Education," Nancy says. "The program hasn't been printed and I can still get you listed as a member if you attend the next meeting. Either that or just send a check."

Deborah takes a sip of her wine and nods.

"The party is going to be fabulous. We've spent a fortune. It's going to be at Linda Davidson's estate. You know her husband, right? You'll have to be there." Nancy smiles venomously at Dan.

"That sounds great," Dan replies.

He's always willing to speak for me, Deborah thinks.

"I'll email the information, to Deborah. I could really use some support," Nancy says. "The new chairwoman is this matronly type who wants us to have a three drink limit. She says she's worried about liability. But I said, isn't that what insurance is for!" Nancy smiles again at Dan to make sure he's still interested in her and then, deeply sighing, she says, "We all know the auction stuff goes for more money after a few cocktails. Malibu is such a wonderful place. We have four children, and at our youngest daughter's school fundraiser the students' art projects were auctioned off for a couple of thousand dollars each."

Deborah finds herself nodding for no reason.

"Do you have any?" Nancy asks.

Deborah has just figured out Nancy means children when Dan interrupts. "We're planning to try soon," he says.

"Don't wait too long. You're not getting any younger," Nancy says and then laughs. She certainly entertains herself, Deborah thinks as she keeps nodding and smiling. Nancy blows an air kiss with her glossy pink collagen- filled lips and leads her husband away from the table.

"What a nice couple," Dan says. "You need to call her, Deborah. It'll be good for you."

Deborah thinks about saying what she thinks might really be good for her, but then stops herself. Actually she doesn't know what would be good for her. She barely survived childhood and then college. Before she knew it she was married. How can she explain to Dan all that she's feeling? She takes another sip of wine and sets it on the table. She decides to try, but then Dan begins to talk about investments he's eyeing. He criticizes his coworkers for being too lazy and his partners for being too greedy. He speaks about mutual friends in Newport, mutual funds, and reminds his wife that he's leaving Friday for a weekend golf trip to Pebble Beach. He suggests they throw a summer dinner party to show off their house and plans a ski trip to Telluride in the winter. Kobe short ribs leave the table, the Black Cod entrée arrives, and they nibble on Passion Fruit sorbet for dessert. Deborah nods. She doesn't reveal what she wants to share. Now, she doesn't want to talk to him about the snakebite or the hospital. Dan pays the bill and they walk out.

Sixteen

Waking up alone in her king bed, Deborah thinks about bodies lying intertwined in a large flowering garden. Dan is gone. It's easier to imagine feeling happy without him. The telephone rings. She rolls over the cool jersey sheets and wishes that it would be Joe. Why didn't she give him her phone number? She would like to go to the beach with him. She'd wear that new black bikini and lie besides him on the hot sand. She longs for him to stroke the inside softness of her thighs. The sun pours through the bedroom window and she imagines the feel of the wet moist sand covering her bare feet.

She answers the phone breathlessly.

"This is Alice Edwards from Santa Monica Hospital," the voice says. "Is this an okay time?"

Deborah feels caught.

"Deborah, I'm looking for information about Amber. I thought that you could help," Alice says.

"Sorry," Deborah says. She doesn't quite know what she's apologizing for. It could be her thoughts of infidelity or just the fact that she knows nothing about Amber.

"Unfortunately, there's an emergency," says Alice. "Off the record, she attempted suicide last night."

Deborah lies back in the bed with the phone still held to her ear. "Is there something that I can do?" she asks.

"Just let me know if you hear anything. She won't give a real last name," Alice says.

Deborah looks out at the ocean. The waves look powerful enough to wash her away.

Seventeen

Deborah paces the house. The laundry baskets are empty. The dishes are washed. The hardwood floors are spotless. When she walks into a guest bathroom the toilet sparkles. She has to keep moving. She walks downstairs into her closet and opens Dan's underwear drawer. The gun is gone.

She removes a pair of his white cotton briefs. She holds them at eye level and shakes them as if a gun might fall out. She tosses them onto the floor. One by one she goes through each piece until the drawer is empty and the underwear is in a heap.

Worried, she walks into the bedroom. She's sick and tired of him. She picks up the phone and lies back on the bed.

"Daniel Miller's office," Ashley says in her annoyingly perky voice.

"It's Deborah. I need to speak to him," she says staring at the ceiling.

"Sorry, he's busy," Ashley, replies cheerfully.

Busy doing what? She sits up and looks around the room. It's only her and the phone and the radio. She clears her throat. "I need to speak to him and no you may not take a message. Patch me through, or I'll see that you're fired," Deborah says, shocking herself.

She feels a rush. Billy Joel is singing Uptown Girl on hold. Why did he leave Christy Brinkley? Or was it the other way around? She tries to remember the story while she waits.

"How dare you embarrass me like that? Ashley's practically in tears," Dan says.

"I don't care. I need to tell you what happened," Deborah says.

"Why didn't you just say, "Ashley, it's an emergency." You sound like a spoiled child. Now I have to deal with consoling her so she can get back to work like the rest of us," Dan says.

"I'm sick being coached... 'Deborah, make sure that you're friendly to Mr. Smith's wife this evening. Deborah, don't wear that red blouse. Deborah, don't tell Mr. Hammond that you disagree with his politics.'

"Watch what you're saying, Deborah."

"You know these people's opinions better than you know yourself," Deborah says. She stands up from bed and crosses the room. She avoids looking into the mirror. She's scaring herself.

"Did you schedule the psychiatrist yet?" Dan says, "I think you need a prescription."

She can imagine Dan sitting at his desk and shaking his head. She faces the window. She watches as the waves break on the deserted beach. "I need lots of things, but medication is not one of them." she replies.

"Are you on your period?" he asks.

She can hear the clicking of his keyboard. She rolls her eyes. "I saved a girl's life."

"What are you talking about? Just calm down," he says.

"This girl has no one. She tried to kill herself," Deborah says.

"I hope you're not suggesting that we pay for her or anything crazy like that. We have enough financial responsibilities," Dan says. "Brooke Shields takes them you know."

She's unable to speak. Even if she could it seems like he's unable to hear what she's saying anyway.

"I'm leaving for the airport," he says. "Why don't you go for a walk on the beach?" The line goes dead. She isn't sure who hung up first. It doesn't really matter anymore.

Maybe growing up in a walled estate gives him the tendency to say things like, "walk on the beach." She doubts that it would be the sort of thing his parents would suggest. Their advice would be to talk things out. According to Dan it would be over-analysis. He doesn't have time for that.

She chooses to walk down the hill. She's at the front door of Horizons, braless and wearing an old UCLA T shirt. She runs her tongue across her teeth and feels the slimy film. She should keep up her appearance. Real winners always give their best, no matter what the situation. Isn't that what the Captain always said? His uniform carefully pressed. She should at least brush her hair. She turns around to leave, but the door opens and she finds herself facing Joe.

"I don't know what I'm doing here," she says and then sees a platinum blonde peering around his shoulder.

"We're about to walk outside. Do you want to wait?" he asks.

Deborah thinks this girl doesn't look ready to walk anywhere in her black patent heels. The convertible Mercedes parked in the driveway with the "Daddy's Girl" license plate frame must belong to her. She tries to regain some composure. "No. I want you to know that Amber attempted suicide," Deborah says. She turns to leave and feels the blonde's glare stab her in the back. Of course he'd have a girlfriend. And I have a husband, she thinks.

Eighteen

At home she finds herself in her bedroom and under the covers. She listens to the hum of Rosa's vacuuming. For once she doesn't care if Rosa thinks she's lazy, but the vacuuming stops and Rosa is calling her.

Reluctantly, she's out of bed, expecting UPS or pest control. Joe is walking downstairs towards her.

Rosa has followed Joe and she's watching from the top of the staircase. "Everything okay?" Rosa asks.

"Yes, this is an old friend of ours," Deborah replies as Rosa raises her eyebrows.

"You didn't have to leave like that," he says.

She feels her heart quicken with his every step. "Like what?" Deborah replies with her arms folded across her chest.

"Like you were uncomfortable," he says when he reaches her.

"Why would I be?" she says, shrugging.

"I know you," he says.

"Everyone seems to think so," she replies.

"So I was wrong?" he asks, stepping towards her.

"I didn't say that."

He looks self-satisfied. "I didn't expect her," he says. They're standing at the open door leading to her bedroom.

"I assume she's a girlfriend or something," Deborah says, feeling jealousy pour over her like an illness.

He looks smaller to her now here in her house, dwarfed by the door. "My ex," he says. "I told her that I'm not moving back in."

Deborah nods and walks into the bedroom. He follows, shutting the door behind him. The window across from her bed is open. The breeze lifts the curtains. She feels that she's already broken an unspoken yet significant marital pact by having him in her room.

"Amber was a mess when you found her," he says looking around the large room.

"I was a mess when you found me too. Remember?" she says, looking down at the beige carpeting. It's clean. Rosa didn't need to vacuum this room today. And who is Rosa to judge?

"You were sick. That happens," he says. "In fact it used it happen to me a lot."

"What did you think of me that day?" Deborah asks, walking towards her bed and sitting down. The white lace bedspread is in a pile on the floor.

"I thought you were beautiful," he says, looking her in the eye. She thinks he's brave. Minutes earlier, he broke up with the blonde.

"So then why did you take off?" he asks, standing across from her.

"It was too awkward," she says, crossing her legs.

"Like me in you and your husband's bedroom," he replies. He's caught her now.

"My husband doesn't spend much time here anymore."
She meets his eyes.

Joe smiles like he knows where he's going.

She likes that. "Did you really think that I was beautiful when I got sick?" Deborah asks.

"I thought that you were a beautiful mess," he says.

"A beautiful mess," Deborah repeats as she slides the three-carat diamond off her left finger. She crawls across the bed and places it in the nightstand where her suicide note had been.

He meets her there and pulls her up to her knees. Her religion had been lost with her mother's absence and her daughter's stillbirth, but now she has found something else. He kisses her hard on the lips. It's better than she imagined. After she feels him inside of her, she knows that there is no turning back. Her life with Dan is over.

Nineteen

"I'm going to leave him," she announces confidently to no one in particular. It's Saturday. Joe sits across from her at the breakfast table. The rain is falling outside on her decking. The massive glass windows are streaked with patterns of falling rain.

"Do you mind if I smoke in here?" he asks.

She says "no," wishing that he wouldn't.

Joe places the cigarette between his moistened lips. Deborah walks into the kitchen and pours coffee. She adds cream, imagining that he would like that. She carries it to him steadily. She returns for a crystal ashtray. She uses her thumbnail to peel off the price tag. A wedding gift used ten years too late.

She had expected to wake up that morning with guilt resting on her chest like a weight. But instead she found relief.

Deborah sets the ashtray down in front of Joe.

"Don't take this wrong, but don't do it for me," he says.

She knows that he means the marriage.

"With my all of my DUIs and legal bullshit, I can't even drive," he says.

"It's okay," Deborah replies and bites the inside of her cheeks. "I can drive."

"You know what I mean, right?" he asks.

She sits and takes a sip of her coffee. It's bitter.

He hates it, she thinks. "Yes, this is for me," she says.

"Besides, won't you miss things here?" he asks, surveying the immaculate home.

"Pilates and acupuncture," she replies. "That's not a reason to stay."

He exhales his smoke and shrugs. The smoke covers her face. "It's not a reason to leave," he replies.

She stares at him. His eyes are the color of the sea on a perfect day but she's unable to see herself reflected in them.

"Let's take a trip, somewhere warm like Mexico," he says.

She smiles.

Joe blows a smoke ring.

She coughs and covers her mouth.

"I'll teach you to dive," Joe says, ashing into the crystal tray.

She imagines them in the deep of the ocean. She runs her fingers through her dark hair and crosses her legs. She wants him again.

He raises his eyebrows. They're blond and blend into his tan skin.

"I'm leaving this marriage for me," she says, convincing herself that it's the truth. She gets up and starts the dishes. Maybe she's more like her own mother than she ever imagined. She feels a closeness to her that she can't remember.

"You've been with him long?" Joe asks.

She nods. "We met when I was twenty-one. I was afraid of being alone." She covers her hands with the wet soapy water. He has eaten everything on his plate. He must have liked her eggs. "I still am," she says.

"Still are what?" he asks while inhaling his cigarette.

"Terrified of being alone," Deborah says. She watches the rain. "Isn't that totally pathetic?"

He walks towards her, still holding onto his cigarette trailing smoke across the room. He kisses her cheek. "No," he says. "But I don't think you need to worry about that anymore."

In her life the plans for her future always outweighed her needs in the present.

Joe puts the burning cigarette out into her sink. He wraps himself behind her, placing his hands on her hips. He smells like Tide. She can feel his erection. It excites her.

"I've got to leave for group, or I'll never hear the end of it," he says.

She looks at the remains of his ashes.

"I'll leave the door open for you tonight," she says.

Joe smiles and walks out as Deborah turns on the faucet and rinses the basin clean.

"Come, give me a kiss," he says standing at the doorway.

Obediently, she goes to him. Her feet crack as she walks. She can hear the rain falling. "I'll get you an umbrella," she says.

He pulls her towards him and kisses her. She tastes cigarettes and coffee.

"I don't need anything. I'll feel clean," he says as he walks into the rain.

She smiles and watches him walk away. He's a Marlboro Man. She sighs, feeling her sins wash away.

Twenty

She's given up searching for Dan's gun. Instead, she's cleaning what remains: long black strands of hair in the bathroom sink, newspapers on the table and underwear on the floor.

The rain stops. She lights a fire. It's the first one that she's made by herself. The smell of pinewood fills the otherwise stale air. She will remember this scent when it's time to leave. This will be a memory to keep. There must be a few, she thinks. She tries to make a mental list that will convince her to stay: food, shelter, and the beach. She can't think of anything else. What she knows is that she had hopes. She is certain of that. Expectations of a nursery to fill, a child to hold, laughter. But she's alone now in a large and empty house.

She looks outside at the grey ocean below. Her fear of falling is gone. She's already landed. At least she hopes that she will.

She's packing and the phone is ringing. She knows its Dan. If she answers then he will say that his cell isn't getting reception up in Pebble Beach. The rates from the room are too high. Whatever, he'll have excuses for not calling yesterday. And yet it doesn't matter anymore.

The phone keeps ringing. If she answers, in the background of their conversation will be other people talking. Maybe it will be the sound of his television or friends laughing at an inside joke. It's better like this, she thinks. She'll make the goodbye quick and painless, like pulling a band aide off an old wound. She'll call him from the road and say, "it's over."

The phone is still ringing. If she tells him now he'll have to walk away from his golf game. Unpleasantness always constitutes the need for absolute privacy. Is that why she's alone all the time?

The phone's quiet. The dishwasher stops.

If she had answered then he would have said, "You'll never make it on your own." His words would have scared her.

She looks into the empty dresser. She was married a year after college graduation. Her father had been proud. My son in-law the lawyer, he told the other pilots. It was a picture that had been framed for as long as she could remember. Education, work, marriage and children: all part of the plan. But whose, she wonders.

It seems like her whole life was laid out like a carefully plotted trip. But it was never an adventure.

Her open suitcase rests heavily on the bed. She's already changed the sheets. Dan doesn't deserve much, but she couldn't let him sleep in the remnants of another man's semen. Her hands are cold and shaking while she zips close the suitcase. There's no going back.

Twenty-One

If there is a phone call to be made then it's this one. She dials Santa Monica hospital and rests her bony elbow on the cold grey marble slab in the kitchen. Alice Edwards's sounds surprised to hear from her.

"Have you been able to help Amber?" Deborah asks.

"We've located her family. In fact, if it's okay with you the mother wants your address so she can send a thank you," says Alice.

"That would be nice," says Deborah. She gives Alice the address of her condo in Palm Springs. Somehow saying it aloud reminds Deborah that she's really moving. She takes a deep breath. "I should be the one to thank you," Deborah says. She is shaking, remembering that it was Alice, not Dan who held her and let her cry after her baby girl died.

Twenty-Two

Deborah awakes to the sound of footsteps descending into her Malibu bedroom. She sits up in bed. It's dark. The small white votive candles that she had left burning have gone out. "Who is it?" she says, unable to see her own hands in the darkness. There's no reply, only rain and the footsteps coming closer. Flashes of white lights up the room and then there's thunder. Joe's stands at the foot of the bed.

"I had my last group," he says.

"Congratulations," she says. Her heart is pounding. She leans across the bed and turns on the lamp. Her negligee is twisted around her petite frame. She pulls up the white duvet up to cover her small exposed breasts.

"You're so beautiful," he says, watching her adjust herself. He makes her believe this. "Still, I wasn't sure about coming."

"Why?" she asks. Her stomach twists into a tight ball.

"Sobriety," he says. "The old me would continue with what we have and not stop. Just as long as it feels good, which it does. But my counselor says..."

"What are you saying?" she asks, already knowing the answer.

"In one year, we'll hook up. We'll take our trip to Mexico."

She wonders what he means by hooking up but doesn't say anything. "I'll be gone," she says.

"What do you mean?" he asks.

"In the morning I'm moving to the desert. I have a place of my own," she says.

"Then I'll meet you there in a year," he says.

"I've seen that movie," she says. She hadn't realized until now that she had needed him to be part of the plan.

"I'll be with my sister in the valley. Her name is Julie Cohen. I'll be there with her and her three sons. Are you cool with waiting for me?" he asks.

She nods, wanting to be cool with something. Her throat clenches tight and she's unable to speak. She will not allow herself to cry.

Joe is smiling and taking off his clothes. She watches him undress and can't help but want him. She goes to turn off the light but he pulls her hand away. "Keep it on," he instructs. "I want you to remember." He's on top of her and enters her quickly. She's ready for him and doesn't want him to stop.

"This isn't the end," he says like it's a promise. She wants him. His body is hard. She moans and feels herself melt. Thunder shakes the room.

In the morning the storm is over and Joe is gone. Maybe she had wanted it this way.

Twenty-Three

The Malibu beach is deserted. One walk along the water and then she'll leave this town. Still, she hopes that something might cause her to change her mind. As she walks, cold sand squishes between her toes. Her footprints are quickly absorbed. Is it that easy to disappear? She wonders. Her own mother left in such a way. It seems to Deborah that it happened like this. But then again, she was only nine.

It's quiet. Too quiet. Waves roll in gently. Her feet go numb. If it were warm enough she'd swim. Or at least she hopes that she would.

She imagines she's pushing her way through the marine layer. Fighting to be seen. Fighting to be heard. Someone must be out there.

In the distance she notices something washed up on the shore. She walks closer. A dead seal is on its side covered in flies. It doesn't smell but she covers her mouth with her hand. It's a natural reflex. How long has it been here? A pattern has appeared. Ahead rows of dead seals line the beach. She can't go on.

"The red algae," a voice calls.

She turns to face a tall ocean front house. An old woman leans over the balcony. She sips from a coffee mug.

Deborah approaches her, but the woman calls out, "Don't come any closer. My dog will attack."

Deborah pauses, terrified of the absent dog. She only hears the waves.

"God damn city was suppose to send someone to clean this mess up," yells the woman.

"Sorry," Deborah replies not knowing what else to say. She has no choice now but to leave.

Twenty-Four

The morning marine layer is still thick. There's no rain and that becomes a sign. Leaving Dan and Malibu is the only chance she has of finding any happiness. Her keys are shaking in her hand. Joe will be sober. She remembers her father coming home in the morning from flying a redeye and pouring him a scotch. It will be better like this. No need to repeat the past. Isn't that the point of leaving?

She looks at the dozen cardboard boxes that she's loaded into the trunk of her Range Rover. From a 6,000 square foot home this is what she can call her own. When she loaded the last of her belongings she shoved the box in the car with the side of her hip. It hurt and she knew it would bruise in the morning.

She climbs into the driver's seat, shivering and sweating. But this was the Malibu lifestyle: In the summer, Santa Ana winds sent flames rushing up the canyons while one day of rain could bring down a hillside. The only road out would end up covered in mud. She had to get out now before it was too late. She turns the key. Her life depends on her leaving. It's a matter of survival.

She looks only at the road leading up and out. Her own mother had left her without a goodbye, so what does a house deserve?

Like most people in Los Angeles, she's most strongly connected to her vehicle. And the car is coming with her.

The boxes in the trunk topple when she turns left onto PCH. There's no stopping to fix them. She's driving fast straight out of town. I'm Rhoda May Rindge, she thinks, a woman who fought the Supreme Court for Malibu and was left with nothing. Deborah presses her foot down harder on the accelerator. It will be a new life.

She stops at a red light. Three homeless men cross in front of her. One pushes a cart full of rags and trash. Two others walk slowly behind. Torn clothing stuck to moist black skin. The light turns green and the car next to her's honks furiously until they pass. She sighs with relief as she continues to drive. Lines of cars are parked alongside the road. The surf is good. Daily responsibilities discarded. Surfers form a line to deliver themselves from reality. Deborah doesn't need the water. She's riding out of Malibu. At sixty-five miles an hour she drives past the city limits. In that one moment she leaves her life. She leaves her body. She leaves the planet. She's in the barrel of the wave.

As she drives, a possible life in Santa Monica flashes by. Women play volleyball in the sand. Some are in a fitness boot camp. None of this looks appealing. She will purposely torture herself no longer. Rollerbladers, cyclists and runners are out on the strand. Deborah keeps pace alongside them in the comfort of her car.

She passes the pier and enters the McClure tunnel. Once she's inside the darkness she's transported into a different existence. Her longings disappear. In her mind, she can see the colors disappearing in the picture of her carefully constructed life. All that remains is an outline. It's like a child's drawing. She begins to fill the drawing with light. Sparkling white and golden light fills the emptiness of that black and white line picture. A higher force is with her.

She emerges from the tunnel and light fills her car. For a moment she's blinded. She puts on her sunglasses and reaches West LA. Traffic has slowed. She's on the fringe. Her breathing feels restricted. She needs to get all the way out. In the distance is Culver City, where working sixty hours a week can afford you a small apartment and a 310 area code.

A sleek black Mercedes station wagon pulls out from the left lane and cuts her off only to slow down again. A small boy in the rear facing child seat sticks out his tongue at her. She raises her middle finger.

Without signaling again, the wagon quickly cuts across two lanes and exits north on La Cienega. The traffic clears and she can breathe.

Deborah passes the rows of California Craftsmans on West Adams. She's almost made it out. Like unarmed soldiers, the houses stand bravely in the face of the 10 freeway. Dilapidated wood helplessly fights the never-ending sound of passing cars. She has lived in Los Angeles for fifteen years and has never seen the inside of one of these homes. Before that she lived lots of places alone with her father. In different homes that always felt alike. None of them like anything here in Los Angeles, though.

She's downtown passing the Staples Center and multimillion-dollar high-rises on her left. Factories and old warehouses on her right, and she's in the middle. She thinks that she's somewhere between the old and the new, the rich and poor.

She looks at herself in the rearview mirror. Her face is pale and fine lines are taking over her once youthful appearance. But Joe had called her beautiful. She is full of possibilities. She's reaching the Inland Empire.

She needs to use the bathroom but will not consider stopping. She can manage. She squeezes her thighs together forcefully. Her cell phone is ringing.

She has come too far to turn back. She will not answer the call. She can make it out. She can be free from LA.

The ring tone sounds like a dying bird. With one touch she commanded all four windows down at once. She can't bear the sound of Dan's voice. She tosses the phone out of the open window and slows down. In the driver's side mirror she watches it hit the empty road and somersault a few times until it lies still. She takes a deep breath and watches a Hummer's front tire crush it. It has died there. Eventually it will be collected with the roadside trash and be given a proper burial. By herself, she laughs out loud.

In the distance is Cabazon, an outpost for the unusual. Unwanted clothing fills the outlet malls. Two life-size dinosaur replicas stand frozen in time in a truck stop parking lot. One wide-eyed brontosaurus and open-mouthed Tyrannosaurus Rex where Pee Wee Herman once perched on his big adventure. Enormous windmills spin furiously in the hot winds like she imagines desert ravers dancing on Ecstasy.

Deborah can't neglect her bladder any longer. The parking lot at the Indian casino is full of recreational vehicles. She exits the 10 and pulls into the dusty road leading to the casino. Everyone is gambling today.

Deborah parks and without hesitation walks towards the tall building. A waterfall empties into a manmade pond next to the entrance. She hopes that she can make it to the bathroom.

Walking inside, she's blasted by cold air conditioning and the smell of cigarette smoke. Deborah glances around nervously. Overweight and tattooed men sit at every card table. Are they watching her? It's hard to tell. They wear dark sunglasses like Tom Cruise in Risky Business.

From every direction Deborah hears falling coins and bells. She's spinning. For a moment she feels like she might actually pass out. She looks up and sees it, a neon orange arrow. The women's room is to the left. She's saved.

Twenty-Five

She follows the tacky red and gold Persian carpeting through the middle of the casino and down a dimly lit hallway. From a distance she hears someone shout out "BLACKJACK!" It too is a sign. Someone here is winning, she thinks. Winners surround me.

She's flooded with relief as the smell of shit greets her. A stubby Indian woman is holding paper towels next to a display of used makeup and perfumes. Deborah smiles at her and opens the stall door. Anxious to relieve herself, she sits on the seat without a cover. She's living on the edge now.

After she's done she washes her hands. She given a paper towel and flashed a toothless smile.

"Having any luck?" The woman speaks through the large hole in the center of her mouth.

Deborah shrugs and opens her purse.

"Keep it for the machines," the woman says.

Deborah nods. She walks into the smoky hall feeling disoriented. Where had she come from? How will she find her car? More importantly, what will she do next? She doesn't know which way to turn. She hears the sound of falling coins and bells. They signal her back into the main casino.

Deborah looks at her watch only from habit. She has nowhere to be and yet she walks towards an exit. Chain smoking eighty year olds in electric wheelchairs monopolize nickel machines. She stops at a dollar slot covered in purple diamonds. She pulls a wrinkled bill from her purse and smoothes it on the side of the cold metal machine. She inserts it and pushes a large yellow button. The symbols spin dramatically. Three diamonds line up across the screen. She stands in the glow of flashing lights. She's won. It doesn't matter how much or how little. Her heart is pounding. Everything is going to work out for her in Palm Springs. Two men in matching leather jackets walk by and congratulate her. She smiles at them. Maybe they're brothers. They wear heavy silver bracelets around their wrists. They offer to buy her a beer.

"No thanks," she says.

She takes the paper ticket from the machine. It says one thousand dollars.

"There's a progressive tournament," says one of the men. Bits of food are caught between his teeth. "You can win a Harley."

"Maybe," she says.

"We'll look for you," the other man says.

They walk away towards the bar and turn back twice as if she'll change her mind.

Deborah goes to the cashier, who seems unimpressed as she quickly counts out the cash with peach acrylic nails and yellowed fingers.

Deborah stuffs her winnings into her purse and walks outside. Her black Range Rover is parked in the distance. She walks quickly and checks back over her shoulder to make certain that no one has followed her.

Twenty-Six

She starts the car, looking forward to arriving at her condo. She pulls out of the casino parking lot and onto a long desert road. Like a Polaroid picture the lines of her new life are slowly beginning to develop, instant by instant. The outline of a body appears and slowly the full self is revealed. She's still not sure whom she'll find once the full portrait is complete.

She reaches an area designated "Windy Point." It's a hazardous turn at the base of a sand-covered mountain. Flashing orange warning signs signal drivers to slow down. She looks to the right and watches a herd of motorcycle riders climb the steep, sandy hill alongside the highway.

She feels like she's in the Wild West.

She sees an oasis of green in the distance. It must be a mirage. Mountains surround the city where she'll live. They'll block the winds and help guard from storms.

I'll make this step on my own, she thinks.

She is wrong.

Part Two

One

Dan Miller pulls his car along the curb in front of his home. He sits and listens to the hum of the motor. He looks in the side mirror and runs his hand through his hair. At least I still have it, he thinks envisioning his balding golf partner, Ralph Turner, a potentially huge client whose endless rants at Pebble Beach left Dan feeling significantly aged at the end of two days.

"Yes, Ralph I certainly see the merits of another Republican in office."

"Absolutely Ralph, and why should the middle class expect so much."

If Dan were a vegetarian and Ralph ordered a boxed hamburger lunch, then Dan would eat one too. And cooked rare.

Dan turns off the engine. But it was worth this, he thinks, looking at his house. He steps out of his car, gathers his belongings from the trunk and walks to his front door. The clean angular lines still appeal to him as much as when he first toured it. A modern house. Simple, without making a statement, yet he imagined that it still spoke volumes about its owners. It projected everything that he valued. Moderation and careful calculation. And yes, he had slightly over-extended himself financially in its purchase, but putting his key in the front lock made his confidence soar. Isn't that what matter most.

In the entrance hall he finds Rosa on her hands and knees polishing the floor.

"Where's Deborah?" he asks.

Rosa stands and shrugs.

Dan mutters and puts down his bags. He is disappointed by the emptiness of the house.

Rosa carries his bags out of the room and he is left alone. He should be used to this. After all, this is how he grew up. Going into his parents' house with a key tied by yarn around his neck.

"Gifted and fiercely independent," his parents labeled him.

"A latchkey child," he read in Time magazine.

His parents shared a successful practice specializing in Christian Marriage and Family Counseling. Weekdays, Daniel would ride the school bus and let himself into the quiet house; he'd make himself a snack and start his homework. His mother arranged her last session to end at 6 pm so that she could make the short drive home, fix dinner and spend "quality time" with her son. His father would tiptoe in by nine to say goodnight. Despite their good intentions, things rarely went as planned. Inevitably his mother would get an emergency call from a patient and end up burning the Stouffers frozen lasagna. Later they would sit at the kitchen table and eat around the burnt ends. She would say things that irritated him. "How did you feel when you struck out in last week's game?" All of the things he tried to put behind him during the week she made him relive through their "quality time." Daniel often pretended to be asleep when his father came in and kissed him goodnight.

"Deborah," he calls. Her name echoes off the walls.

Sunlight shines in through the open window. He hears the waves crash on the shore.

They had fought. Now he regrets what he can't remember he said. The solution will be to take her out to dinner tonight. A new restaurant opened last week at the west end of town.

Dan calls for Deborah again, trying to use a steady voice despite his disappointment.

Rosa returns to the kitchen. He opens the refrigerator and closes it.

"You need dish detergent," Rosa says.

"I'll let Deborah know."

Rosa shrugs and walks away.

He walks downstairs. Something has changed in their bedroom. Her bedside table, usually littered with paperback books, is empty. The bed is perfectly made; she hasn't napped today. Dan tries to recall the exact words of their last telephone conversation but can't. He walks into the closet and sees that her side is empty.

For a moment, he stops breathing.

Two

In the morning Deborah gets out of bed and stubs her big toe on the dresser. She had bought it and some other furniture at a consignment store a few years ago. Cursing, she bends over the sink and splashes cold water on her face. Reality is slowly penetrating. She looks at herself under the glare of fluorescent lighting. The image is unfamiliar. She unwinds a strip of toilet paper and dries her skin.

There's a dead cricket and a bottle of Tylenol on top of the sink. She opens the Tylenol and pops two, chasing them with a cupped handful of sink water. She rolls her shoulders backwards and bends her neck side to side. She brushes her teeth with her forefinger. A rubber band around her wrist has left a deep imprint overnight. She uses it to secure her hair into a loose bun.

She turns to face the mirrored closet, startled by her own reflection. It's the same black hair and green eyes but the face is unfamiliar. The years had not hardened her like they had Dan. His skin grew lined and tight. Her own face looks round and soft. She judges her arms as flabby, her breasts drooping and her butt sagging. The discomfort makes her queasy. She slides the closet open mostly to get away of her own reflection. She suddenly sees herself as weak.

Her weakness is so obvious now. In her hospital room she could've argued with Dan when he walked away. Instead, she sat stone-faced underneath a cross and facing a TV. She thought then it was an act of strength to let him go. She was wrong.

Most of her clothing has fallen off the hangers and piled on the carpet in a giant heap. The rest of her wardrobe remains in boxes piled up by the front door. She pulls on a pair of jeans from the floor and savors the leftover smell of cigarette smoke from the casino. Winning a thousand dollars was a sure sign of something.

She walks the dimly lit hallway and down the stairs. There's a stack of mail already waiting for her. It's like a welcome mat. Catalogues and junk mail spread out over the tiled floors. It was as if the solicitors expected her to wind up living here.

She walks into the kitchen. Dust is everywhere. She never even said goodbye to Rosa, she thinks.

Deborah moves quickly through each room in the condominium in an attempt at cleaning. When she reaches her bathroom, she leans over the bathtub and scrubs it with Comet and water. The smell from the cleaner burns her nose and makes her dizzy. As she stands, the small white tiled bathroom tilts. She steadies herself on the chrome towel bar. Putting all of her weight on it causes one side to break from the drywall, leaving a hole. The yellow velour towel slides down to the floor. Bending to pick up the towel, she sees a brown insect sprint to the opposite corner. She crawls toward the toilet and wads up a handful of toilet paper. The bug is next to the bathtub now; its black head and long antenna are facing her. It has wings and it's the size of a very small mouse. She knows it's a date bug. The toilet paper isn't large enough to smother it.

She jumps to her feet and runs down the hall to her room. On her bedside table is a paperback book on meditation practices. Without hesitation she grabs it and goes in for the kill. When she returns to the bathroom, the bug is gone. She's rooming with the roaches now.

She sets the meditation book on top of the toilet just in case. She'll be ready next time.

Three

Dan sits on the edge of the kitchen barstool. Deborah has been missing for 24 hours. No one answers her cell. All night he paced the house and wondered what to do. It is a situation he never imagined. At five thirteen am he realized rather slowly and pathetically that she didn't have any friends or family for him to call. And it was at this point that his anger turned into fear.

He thinks that she's threatened him with this before but he can't be sure. The last cup of coffee has made his hands shake. He picks up the mug and takes another sip. It's cold.

Rosa left yesterday after he yelled at her, demanding to be told where Deborah went. Rosa slammed the door behind her when she left. He watched her from the window as she drove away in her green minivan. Now he regrets how he embarrassed himself. He let his emotions get the better of him. He can never face Rosa working for him again. Even when Deborah returns, Rosa will need to be permanently laid off. Maybe he'll find Deborah a companion of some sort. Someone who could clean and help keep her company during the days. Rosa's English was terrible anyway.

He reaches for the phone but knows that there is no one that he would consider calling. His business relationships are strictly that. He credits himself for having such a high level of professionalism.

Certainly he could call his parents in Florida. After all, they are experts in such situations. But their over eagerness to share in the intimate details of his life makes them an even less appealing option.

"And how is your sex life?" asked his father at a celebratory dinner. He'd just introduced Deborah as his fiancé!

"We're looking forward to sharing in the happiness of your marriage," his mother toasted.

They clinked glasses. Dan rolled his eyes at Deborah. He'd have to keep his parents at a distance. He was firm in his decision that they should remain to California. After posing for the wedding photos in his parents' spacious backyard, his mother loudly encouraged both Dan and his beautiful new bride to call her "back line" at any time. She would always be available to help counsel them through any of their future problems. Afterwards, in their honeymoon suite, rubbing Deborah's sore feet, he made her promise to never disclose herself or any of their business to his parents.

"They'll dissect you," he said. Her long black hair was pulled up elegantly, revealing the delicate bones of her neck and shoulders. She had thrown her arms around him and repeatedly kissed him.

"You have me all to yourself. Don't worry so much," she said.

Was he now only imagining that these moments had passed between them? All of the times when he felt so sure that they understood each other so basically that they didn't even need to speak?

Dan rests his head on the countertop. The cold marble feels good against his forehead. He should already be downtown. There is work to be done but he can't move. He remembers when he first met her. How she looked up at him with her doe like eyes from her book in the university commons.

"I can help you with that," he offered, unsure of how else he could approach her for the first time. There were girls before her, of course, who would anxiously follow him back from the bar to his off campus apartment, most of them had been better lovers than Deborah, who lay stiffly beneath him.

Before her there had been opportunity. Girls anxious to please him and show off newly gifted plastic tits. Girls who could still make him hard if he thought long enough about them. They came from families with money and hyphenated names. But, still he wanted Deborah. Perhaps because she was so different from the others. At least she seemed to be so then. Now he's not sure who he's married. A pretty undergrad with long black hair, she reminded him of a ballet dancer in one of the productions that his mother had dragged him to as a boy. Deborah was younger looking than her peers and in his opinion all the more beautiful. He had been disappointed, even shocked, when she revealed to him that she was not a virgin. But her ineptitude in bed made it a forgivable offense.

"Don't leave me," she would cry to him after they had sex. She told him about her childhood. The mother who abandoned the family to "find herself." Her father who was rarely home and when he was how he'd bury himself in books about mechanical things. Flight Simulation. All of the things that didn't interest her.

Her father could fix anything broken: a leaking faucet, wire an electrical short, spark a gas oven. He maintained an organized garage, with parts labeled to make certain repairs. Her time with her father was something that couldn't be repaired. Dan thought it was best left in the past. Why retell something that can't be improved? Dan would never leave her. Never ask her more than what she wanted to share.

For her part, she let him simply be. She never said things like "let's talk about our feelings." So while his college friends were practicing Frisbee golf or attempting to convince him to invest in their dot com businesses, Deborah's very existence made him stay the course that he had always envisioned for himself long before they met. Yes, there was a brief temptation to give up law school for a more exciting and unknown future in Silicon Valley. But what he wanted then and what he wanted now was stability. Feelings that remained unchanged. He looks at the clock on the microwave. A steady and consistent law practice.

He throws his coffee mug across the room and watches it break on the marble floor. He stands and walks the perimeter of the family room again hoping to find a clue. He slicks his hair back and curses under his breath.

He walks out on the balcony and looks down at the ocean below. It's a long way down from where he stands. The lone paddle boarder seems to be mocking the life that Dan chose for himself as he slices a straight path through the water.

"Kidnapping," Dan says aloud. As if the word alone would help make him feel better.

He walks inside and picks up the phone. He dials the police. "I'd like to report a missing person," he says to the operator.

He holds for an officer who speaks to him with sympathetic sarcasm. "They can get like this. Give her some time," says the cop as if he offers this advice everyday. "A report won't help your situation and besides, there is the 48 hours which you'd have to wait anyway."

Dan cracks his neck from side to side. "But, there could be some sort of foul play involved here. He finds himself defending her. "She's not that type," he says.

"In any case, she's not a child," says the officer.

Dan pauses. "There's nowhere for her to go," Dan says as an image of the desert flashes through his mind. Without saying anymore he hangs up the phone feeling suddenly foolish. It's 11:02 am. He can't believe that it took him this long to figure it out. He must be losing his edge. Deborah's melodrama has affected him. His emotional state is not acceptable. He can still make it downtown in time for his lunch meeting.

Dan clears his throat, finding that the fear is gone and anger has returned.

Four

Desert blocks are longer to walk than city ones. Although they may measure the same distance, people provide temporary distraction. I hate him, Deborah says to no one. How could I have wasted those years? Still, he is my husband. What happened to our vows? Sand pours in the sides of her shoes and burns the bottoms of her feet. She walks quickly, hoping to make the pain stop.

She's thought a walk would help her forget about calling Dan. But there is her nagging sense of obligation to let him know where she's gone. The good girl inside of her won't let her act this irresponsibly without some guilt.

The sun is bright. Two days ago, she'd left the casino and drove away in what she'd considered to be her own car. She was free. She wasn't bound for her father's old white colonial or her husband's modern monstrosity. She'd pulled into a parking space assigned to her. She'd live in a condominium built in the 1970's with thick yellow stucco.

This condo was to be their weekend retreat. Deborah purchased it with her small inheritance. She'd thought that Dan would golf and she would sit by the pool. It was an anniversary gift to Dan. But he had never liked it. He said that it reminded him of Florida. "Too many old people and nothing to do." The truth was that it reminded him of home.

But to her the desert felt free. She could see everything in front of her. It felt safe.

"I can't breathe here," Dan had told her after a colleague bought a weekend home in a country club 20 miles to the east. "If you really want to come here then we should get a bigger place. Maybe I'd like it more," he said. Money could solve any problem.

It never happened and the condo was largely forgotten except during tax season.

Now Deborah steps on a low bush. It crackles and breaks beneath her feet. She walks out of the desert and into the town. There is a liquor store a few blocks up. The best part about being alone is that there is no one to argue the point of what to do next. Not that she'd ever disagreed with Dan's plans out loud before now. Still, the internal struggle was always deep inside of her.

A few cars drive past and for a moment she thinks about hitching a ride. It's something that she had never considered before. The Captain would have kept her locked in her room for a year. After her mother left them, she felt his eyes watching her even when he wasn't around. It wasn't until one year after he died that she felt the stare disappear. In a way, his dying felt like a relief, and she often wonders if this makes her a horrible person.

She'd always anticipated his death. She always thought his life would come to a dramatic end: an airplane crash, a suicide, murder. A sudden massive heart attack seemed too mundane.

Her feet hurt and she's thirsty. She imagines that the tall palm trees are actually waving to her as their fan leaves sway in the breeze. Maybe I've lost my mind, she thinks. I'm a madman lost in the desert. Madwoman, she corrects herself.

She walks past businesses boarded up with large plywood sheets and shops selling souvenir t-shirts and plastic high heels for children. A Mexican restaurant serves a patio full of hungry tourists, their skin the color of salmon. Deborah watches a group of women drinking Margaritas at an outdoor table. She tries not to get caught staring but she can't help inspecting them. Why are we such mysteries to each other? Maybe it's because we're often mysteries to ourselves. She thinks of women she's known over the years and regrets the friendships that she let silently fade away. One of the women at the table wears a white baseball cap with a lace bridal veil. The women laugh and Deborah feels left out of a joke.

The old man behind the counter at the Liquor Barn looks up from his paper and nods to her. She returns the gesture and looks around, evaluating what can fit into two paper bags. She's operating on a new instinct as she moves down the crowded aisles. It's called survival.

She gathers some essentials for the kitchen: bread, milk, eggs and juice. Maybe tomorrow she'll go to a real market but for today this will suffice. The man bags her items. She pays him, leaves the store and walks the rest of the way home.

She's thirsty and decides to walk back and get a drink. But when she walks inside she surprises herself by reaches for the phone instead of a glass.

She dials Dan's office.

"I'm staying in the desert," she says to him, feeling nervous.

"You don't know what you're doing," Dan says, in a professional and steady voice. "Divorce is for losers."

Her hands shake and she hangs up the phone. It wasn't worth calling. She walks across the condo and begins to unpack a box left in the living room. It's filled with papers and books that she collected on her way out of her Malibu house. At the bottom of the box she finds her camera bag. She takes out the Canon camera that she'd saved for in college and looks though the viewfinder. Her world has become so tiny over the past years. Maybe Dan would've preferred that I killed myself, she thinks. She sets the camera on the coffee table and feels a sense of relief that she hadn't given him the pleasure.

Without wanting to, she remembers the first weekend she and Dan had spent here it rained. Flash flood warnings interrupted the televised golf tournament.

"We shouldn't have left LA," Dan said from the sofa.

Deborah was in the living room pushing a hot iron over a clean white sheet.

"What's the point of a three hour drive in traffic to come and sit inside all weekend," he said, turning the television off and facing her.

The rain pounded the rooftop. She sprayed a bottle of a lavender scent over the smooth sheet.

Deborah laughs now. How stupid to think that a certain smell could fix everything. How pathetic.

Five

He will not run to her. That would be something a lesser man would do. He could get back in his car and drive to the desert. But he still has his pride. His ego will not allow him to look weak.

Dan straightens his tie as he walks into the busy downtown restaurant for lunch. He's a few minutes late but he'll blame the traffic on PCH. It's an acceptable and even enviable excuse in Los Angeles. No, he will not go to the condo even though he is certain that she is there. His ego will not allow him to go after her.

The lunch crowd is noisy, gathering like cattle at the bar. Dan nods at the hostess, who smiles at him even while attempting to reason with a disgruntled customer. Dan holds himself erectly as he walks through the place. He feels the admiring stares especially from women as he passes their tables, and feels overcome with anger at Deborah. How dare she! Every booth is full, including his.

"Construction, seems it will never end," he says to the group meeting him for a celebratory lunch. They smile.

Two of the men slide out of the booth to make room. His tardiness has left him with an inside seat next to Marissa Wilkins, a dumpy newly hired junior partner. He moves towards her hesitantly. Sitting next to her he finds himself afraid that her fat thighs will touch him at some point during their meal.

"We couldn't toast without you," says Davidson, a scrawny and all too eager assistant.

Greenberg, his only professional equal at the table, gives him an all- knowing look. But Steve has no idea what's running through Dan's mind. Everything they see is completely false: the cheers, clinking of the glasses, the pats on the back and orders of seventy-five dollar fillet cuts. Despite all of this congratulating, he longs to throw his plate across the room.

Back at the office, he shuffles papers around his desk, moving things from one pile to the next in a futile attempt to stay busy. Checking his email, calling in his inept assistant every few minutes to give her something else insignificant and menial to do. It is the only action that seems to give him a sense of relief. Everything else is fuzzy and unfocused. And finally, when she walks out to go home for the day, he lays his head on his desk. Never before has he felt so ineffective at work. Not even after the thing with the miscarriage when everyone offered their sincerest sympathy and told him to go home. He'd stayed, feeling in the office a sense of focus that he couldn't find anywhere else. In fact, last year his performance soared. Besides, it was better to be useful at work than back at the house, dealing with his ineptitude at disassembling the crib and putting the rocking chair into storage. He paid a day laborer to do it, assuring himself that these baby items would be retrieved again one day. When Deborah told him she was ready, they would try again. In the meantime, he would not push her into anything and he would bury himself in work.

His eyes are closing; he's almost asleep on his desk when Steve Greenberg walks in unannounced. Immediately, Dan sits up straight and slicks his hair back.

"What's up?" Steve says.

"Setting the dates for Ralph Turner," he says.

"Thanks for taking that meeting," Steve says. "He wears people down. I caught him moving his ball at Sherwood last month."

"I hope you didn't call him out on it," Dan says, feeling that he's being inspected.

Steve's black bushy eyebrows move closer together. "Are you okay?" Steve says. "You didn't seem yourself at lunch."

And who is Steve to judge, Dan wonders. Steve with his potbelly and cheap suits.

"Everything is fine," Dan says standing and stretching behind his desk. His neck cracks when he moves it to the side.

"Never seen you tired. You're an animal. In fact never heard of you missing a day yet, " Steve says.

Dan knows he should take this as a compliment but finds himself irritated. "I told you things are fine. Drop it," he says.

"Take it easy, man," Steve says, lowering himself into the chair facing Dan's desk as if he sees this weakness as an invitation to intervene.

If there was someone who he'd confide in it might be Steve. A peer, yet someone who is really unable to compete.

Dan sits back down, still embarrassed from losing his cool. "I'm having some issues with Deborah," he says.

Steve smiles. "My second marriage was temporarily saved by a nice two week vacation at Four Seasons. It doesn't matter which one. They kiss your ass there and the women, love those places."

Dan remembers Steve's holiday card. A glossy photo with Steve and his now ex-wife posing poolside with their four dogs. Hadn't he and Deborah laughed when they saw it? Or was he the only one laughing? He can't remember anymore.

"I don't know," Dan says.

Steve leans back and rests his hands across his stomach. "I'd suggest therapy but it never worked that well for me. That and it's a little passé now, don't you agree?"

"Absolutely," Dan says. He has long since rejected therapy, his parents, and organized religion. But what remains? He stands up and gathers his things.

"Well, call me if you need to talk or a drink. I'm an expert at dysfunction," Steve says.

"It's nothing like that," Dan says.

He pats Steve on the shoulder as he leads him out of his office. The hallway is dark. They're the only ones left on the floor. Dan looks out of the window. The high-rises illuminate downtown Los Angeles. He imagines Deborah alone in the darkness of that depressing condominium.

Dan gets in the elevator. Serves her right! "Keep your head up," Steve says as the doors close between them.

Six

Sunlight pours into every crack and corner of the tiny living room. It is now evident that the weather is not controlled by her disposition. In Malibu, she feared that she had somehow been responsible for the constant marine layer over her house.

Deborah changes into a bathing suit and walks outside. At the pool she watches as two brown, leathered ladies float on foam rafts. Deborah sits at the pool's edge and dips her feet into the cool water. She inhales deeply, hoping to conjure a memory involving summertime and childhood fun from the vapors rising off the hot cement. Instead she feels nothing and it frightens her.

She lowers her body slowly into the water, a chlorinated baptism. This is what I need, she tells herself: a ritual, a sense of faith, something to believe.

During her last days in Malibu she thinks that she found the answers in Joe. It wasn't meant to last but still meeting him helped move her forward. What will be the next step?

Deborah holds her breath and submerges herself under the water's sleek surface, eyes shut tight, and thinks, please help me live, and then speaks the words in a bubbly underwater language. She waits for confirmation but sees only blackness. A constriction clutches her chest. She pushes herself up desperately from the bottom and rises to the surface. Her hair is slicked back and her face wet. She wipes her eyes. When she opens them she sees Amber, standing motionless by the side of the pool. Her straw colored hair is pulled into a ponytail and her skin is the color of snow. She's a ghost, Deborah thinks as she gasps for air.

"You're the only one that I could trust," Amber says, her eyes so intensely focused on Deborah that it frightens her.

"You shouldn't be here, you need help," Deborah says, rising out of the water, tying her towel around her waist.

"That's what they wanted you to believe," says Amber. "It part of their conspiracy. I knew that you'd escape."

The two women on rafts remove their hot pink protective eyewear in unison to turn and stare. Deborah can sense their disapproval. It makes her anxious. "Lets go inside," she says and motions for Amber to follow.

Seven

"You shouldn't be here," Deborah says again. She isn't alone anymore. "Do you want a drink?" she asks, feeling annoyed though always mindful of manners.

Amber shakes her head. "My community turned on me and my family wants me dead," she says, standing in the center of the small living room, tears falling from her face.

Deborah walks into the bare kitchen. She fills a glass with sink water. It's all that she has to offer. Why and how is this girl here? If only it had been Joe.

She hands Amber the glass and sits on the brown leather sofa. It's cold against her skin and she's covered in goose bumps. "It's not right, you being here," Deborah says shaking her head.

"You're so beautiful and kind," Amber says, handing Deborah back the emptied glass.

"Do you want more?" Deborah asks.

Amber shakes her head. Tears stream down her face; she totters to the couch and falls helplessly into Deborah's arms. "The nurse, Alice, she said that you were special. She

gave me your address and that's how I found you again."
She kneels in front of Deborah, her voice trembling as she
speaks.

Amber had followed her here. Like a child, Deborah
thinks. A poor lost girl. Although she is not little. At nine-
teen Amber is both taller and broader than Deborah.

Amber cries against Deborah's wet bathing suit.

"Okay," Deborah says, feeling herself softening, "you
can stay until we get things sorted out for you."

Amber sits up and smiles. Her teeth are perfect and
white. Someone invested a lot of money in those teeth,
Deborah thinks. She studies Amber's face, searching for the
dirty girl she rescued from the side of the road, but with
her clean and white complexion she's now a completely different person.

"I won't let you down," Amber says.

Here is one piece of the past that Deborah can hold
onto.

Later that night, Deborah lies in bed and stares up into
the popcorn ceiling. Amber is asleep on the living room
sofa. Deborah has gone to check on her twice to make sure
that she was covered up properly. After all, she's someone's
daughter. Maybe I'd have been a good mother after all,
Deborah thinks. She could've read bedtime stories, tucked
her under the covers and kissed her good night. She wonders where she would be if she didn't miscarry.

Deborah turns over and tries to sleep but feels a rising
pain spreading throughout her body that she's trying her
best to ignore. The window across from her bed is open.
She hears crickets, horny males calling out for a mate. She
thinks of Joe before falling asleep.

In the morning she wakes to the smell of bacon. The
small kitchen table has been set with white plastic plates

and orange paper napkins. There are dishes of scrambled eggs, bacon, muffins, yogurt, and pancakes. "I wasn't sure what you liked so I got it all," Amber says. She is in the kitchen squeezing an orange into a glass.

"Where did this come from?" Deborah asks, fully awake and feeling ravenous.

Amber explains that she got up at dawn and walked the three miles to the grocery store.

"But so much, how did you get it all back here?" Deborah asks.

Amber laughs, "I'm stronger than I look," she says while throwing the orange rinds into the trash. She hands the fresh squeezed juice to Deborah who takes the glass and drinks it all eagerly.

They sit at the table together. "I'll move in with my cousin," Amber says, her mouth full of food.

Deborah is too busy filling her plate to care about her bad manners.

"Her roommate leaves at the end of the month," Amber continues, "If I could stay here till then, I'd be safe."

Deborah was planning to protest after she finished chewing her bacon. It's the best thing she's eaten in days. And then the doorbell rings. Suddenly Amber is standing and pleading, "Don't let them take me back. I'll die there." She runs into the bathroom and slams the door.

Deborah thinks the girl is being ridiculous, annoyed at having to leave her breakfast. The man at the door introduces himself, "Detective Mike Williams," he says, extending a hand. She shakes it reluctantly. He appears to be Deborah's age, tall and thin with slicked back black hair. He reminds her of Dan. Without an explanation, she feels violated by his presence.

"What can I do for you?" she asks.

"I'm looking for a missing person," he says and pulls a wallet-sized photo from his pocket and hands it to her. Amber's wearing a graduation cap and gown with the tassel turned to the side. Deborah remembers herself at eighteen. Why wasn't she able to find her own independence then?

The officer taps his foot impatiently. Deborah finds this rude and irritating.

"Sorry, can't help you," she says staring down the face of authority. She feels exhilaration at telling such a bold lie. This is easier than I imagined, she thinks. "I did help her out in Malibu and at the hospital in Santa Monica but I haven't seen her since."

"If you hear anything," he says and hands Deborah his card. He writes his cell phone number on the back and she rolls her eyes.

"The family's following every possible lead. They have a lot of money and they're desperate to get her back," he says.

Deborah knows about this: desperation and money is a dangerous combination. Amber must be telling the truth after all. Amber and I are more alike than I realized, Deborah thinks. We both want to be free to start a new life. There's nothing wrong with that. Is there?

"Sure," she says to the detective and closes the door in his face.

Eight

Amber opens the bathroom door a crack and looks around.

"He's gone," Deborah says, returning to her breakfast as Amber runs out and throws her arms around her neck, hugging her so tightly it hurts. "You're so cool," she says.

Deborah takes a bite of cold eggs and relishes the idea that someone thinks she's cool.

Amber insists on washing the dishes. Deborah takes her meditation book from the bathroom and begins to read on the sofa. The sound of clanking in the kitchen fills her with enormous relief. She breathes in deeply like the book suggests and searches her mind for things to be grateful for.

"So what do you do for fun?" Amber says, walking into the living room and interrupting Deborah's thoughts about Joe.

"I'm not sure yet," Deborah replies honestly. She watches Amber dry her hands on her torn jeans.

"How about more swimming?" Amber asks.

"No thanks. You can borrow a suit though. I have an extra one in the top drawer," Deborah says, returning to her book and the moment.

"I'm fine," Amber says.

Deborah is concentrating on her inhalations. She notices that in the past she has been accustomed to holding her breath. Things are changing. When she looks up, Amber is walking out the front door naked.

"What are you doing?" Deborah shouts as the book falls into her lap.

"Swimming," Amber replies as the door closes behind her.

Deborah stands and the book falls to the floor. My God, she thinks, what have I gotten myself into? And I just lied to the police, so there's no one left to turn to.

Deborah reaches the community pool, relieved to find no one's outside. Is there anyone else even here? She wonders. Still, she opens the gate and it slams shut behind her, rattling in its metal groove.

Amber moves beneath the surface like an underwater ballerina. The palm trees reflected on the pool seem to sway from her graceful movements. Deborah crouches, her toes warmed by the hot cement as Amber comes up for air.

"Get out." Deborah speaks softly despite her anger. She does not want a scene.

"Swimming is like flying," Amber says, treading in the deep end. "Come in. It feels amazing."

"There are certain rules," says Deborah, feeling a deep stretch in her thighs as she stands up straight and looks down. She sounds like her father.

"Trust me, they don't matter," Amber says before disappearing again.

Deborah is left facing her own reflection. "It matters to me," she says to no one.

Amber resurfaces at the shallow end. Slowly, she climbs out of the pool, her naked body glistening in the sun. Deborah can't help but watch. It is a body that has not yet begun to betray itself. Her pale naked skin is flawless. She moves effortlessly around the pool and out of the gate. Deborah follows the trail of wet footprints, which evaporate quickly on the cement. "This is not acceptable," she hears herself saying. Beneath the anger is a level of jealousy. She can see this in herself. She knows that's a feeling shared by many women when they look at what could have been a younger version of themselves. Time and what was once possible is now lost. She thinks of the years wasted with Dan.

Inside the condo, Deborah picks up the discarded pile of clothes by the front door and throws them at Amber. "Use the washing machine," Deborah says. Her head hurts. So much for playing it cool, she thinks. All at once the condo feels like it's shrinking, too small for the both of them. "And I've changed my mind about our arrangement," Deborah says. The walls are closing in. Maybe Dan was right not to like this place?

Amber is holding her clothes to her chest. Water is dripping onto the shag carpeting. She doesn't speak. Tiny goose bumps cover her naked flesh.

Deborah's desperately tries not to feel concerned about the fact that the girl could catch a cold. "Let me get you something to wear," she says, walking towards her bedroom and shaking her head.

"Do you wish to get rid of me?" Amber calls after her. Deborah doesn't reply; she returns carrying a towel and a soft pink cotton sundress. "Shower," she says. "And get dressed."

"I'll be gone after that," says Amber, her eyes downcast.

Deborah shakes her head. "No, you won't," she replies as she goes back to the sofa and picks her meditation book off the floor. There's nothing wrong with this condo. Dan isn't right about anything, she thinks and sits. Besides, who could have seen Amber's naked body anyway? The only people living here must be either very old or very gay, she rationalizes.

That night, however, Deborah can't sleep. She lies in her bed with the door to her room locked. The walls are thin and she hears Amber laughing and talking to herself. Deborah watches the clock. Her heart is pounding. She is wishing for Joe or the gun that she left in Malibu. Only when it is finally quiet at four am does she allow herself to fall asleep.

Nine

Maybe it was his last phone conversation with Steve that left him unable to face going back to the office. The alcohol induced confession: Deborah had moved out, wouldn't take his calls, and had hired a lawyer.

The following day, Dan hadn't been able to get out of bed. What made him succeed at work was the ability to keep his composure. Now he felt unable to do so. He called his assistant and told her he was sick. This was almost the truth, wasn't it?

Struggling to get up, he lifts his robe from the floor. He puts it on. It smells like stale beer. He walks upstairs and looks around the house. It tells his story. Trash litters the kitchen counter tops, dirty dishes in the sink, and the broken mug's shards on the floor. He turns around and walks back downstairs to his bedroom.

The sun has set when Steve shows up unannounced. "Quite the cliché bachelor pad," Steve says, inviting himself him in and settling onto the hard sofa.

Dan scuffles nervously around the room and offers him a drink. "I fired the housekeeper," he says.

"Obviously," Steve says.

Dan pours him a tall Jack and Coke from the bar, then hands it to him and sits down.

"I was on my way to Moonshadows, thought I'd pick you up," Steve says.

"Not tonight," Dan says.

"I've been there," says Steve, "and I know what'll cure you. Besides, it worked for Mel, didn't it," he says and laughs at his own joke. Mel Gibson left Moonshadows right before his infamous drunk driving escapade.

"That's encouraging," Dan says.

"This is LA and you're a rich man. Trust me, this is not a tragic situation," Steve says.

"Alright. I don't feel like fighting anymore. Besides, you're a good lawyer." He walks downstairs and changes his clothes. Maybe Steve is right about going out for a drink? It couldn't hurt, Dan decides.

Dan tucks his shirt into his jeans and follows Steve inside. Moonshadows is five miles from his house but he has never been here before. They step out onto a large outdoor deck ten feet up from the sand. Fog obscures the view but he hears the waves crashing. Steve pays a scantily clad hostess to lead them to one of the few available cabanas. It's set with a low table and two sofas. This is not the college bar of the 1990's. A DJ in the corner is playing music that Dan doesn't recognize, but it's not Kurt Cobain.

Steve orders drinks and the two men recline on the sofa. Dan watches people mingle. The crowd is full of sculpted women.

Dan raises his glass to Steve when the drinks arrive. "The next ones are on me," he says, smiling at the cocktail waitress and slipping her his platinum American Express. Steve gestures towards a group of three women to come join them. Unbelievingly, Dan watches them saunter slowly towards the cabana, laughing and whispering to one another. Is everything this easy now? He wonders. He feels himself grow eager. The blond, with large plastic breasts and a tiny waist, catches his eye.

"Trust me, she's good to go," Steve says, leaning in.

Dan already images himself on top of her in his bed.

The girls arrive with the second round of drinks. "What can we get you beautiful ladies?" Steve asks. The blond speaks to the cocktail waitress and she steps closer to the light. "Three cosmos," she says. Her skin is pulled tight across her face. She does not have a visible line or wrinkle but it is clear that she is close to fifty.

"And you?" the waitress asks Dan.

"Nothing, thanks," he says slumping further into the sofa. The other two blonds sit beside Steve and the fifty year old joins Dan.

"Come on, doll, have a drink with me," she says to Dan. There's no doubt that at one time this woman was extremely pretty, beautiful even. Her features are perfect, but now she works hard to maintain a façade that doesn't quiet pass for the real thing.

"All right, another Jack and Coke," Dan says to the waitress.

Steve talks about the law firm while Dan watches. The three women all look alike, wearing tight youthful clothes that show off their defined bodies, light natural-looking makeup. They have smooth shiny hair. But they are certainly not the twenty year olds they wish to be. And it makes them scary. Maybe I closed my eyes while fucking them, Dan thinks.

"We can move this party to my friend here's house," Steve says. It's just a few miles away and it has an amazing view of the coastline. I can fit you petite things into the backseat of my Porsche," he adds.

"Sounds fun," says the girl to his left. "But my house is just a few steps down from here and on the sand. We can walk."

And it's a more impressive address, Dan thinks.

The fog has rolled into the cabana. The waitress returns with the drinks and the sound of the waves drown out the music and other partiers. "Are you coming?" the blond next to Dan asks.

Steve speaks for him. "Absolutely. You see, ladies, my friend here is mending a broken heart. Maybe one or all of you can help him."

The women giggle.

"Perfect, I'm mending mine too," says the blonde with beachfront real estate. My husband is punishing me by not having sex with me. He's pissed about the last AMEX bill. And he's out of town."

Dan stands and excuses himself.

"We'll be right back," Steve says and follows him across the deck and into the restaurant.

"I'm calling a cab," Dan says.

"Are you crazy?" Steve says. "Look Dan, welcome to the times. This isn't 1950."

Dan pulls out his Blackberry.

Steve shakes his head. "Don't worry about it. I'll drive you home," he says.

"What about them?" asks Dan.

"Don't you get it? That's the beauty of it all. You don't have to worry about them. Trust me. The women out here, they take care of themselves. They don't need you or anyone," Steve says as they walk through the dark parking lot.

Dan thinks of Deborah as he gets into the passenger seat. She'd been private about sharing her feelings. He thought he'd been respectful by not talking about the miscarriage. He certainly didn't want to pry like his parents always did. Had he made a terrible mistake by assuming that she'd be ok? If she'd stayed in Malibu, would she have turned into a woman like the ones he'd just met? Were money, sex and youth the only things that mattered here?

Steve starts the car and they speed off up the highway toward to his house.

"How fast have you taken this thing?" Dan asks.

"One twenty on a road trip to Vegas," Steve says.

"Let's see," Dan says.

The engine's noise fills the otherwise dark empty road. Dan close his eyes and imagines that they're flying. Steve slows down to make the turn up toward Dan's house. "Maybe I should get one of these," Dan says.

"I'll introduce you to my dealer," Steve says. He's driving slowly now, and the silence makes Dan eager to get out. Steve stops the car in front of Dan's house. "Do you want to come in?" Dan asks. He prays silently that Steve will say no.

"I'm going back to Moonshadows. There's still hope for me," Steve says. "I'll just tell them that you got sick."

Dan gets out of the car. "You won't be lying," he says.

Ten

At noon, Amber is still asleep. The living room curtains are closed but Deborah is certain that it must be sunny outside. She is tiptoeing around the condo picking up dirty clothes and making Folgers instant coffee, envying how soundly Amber is able to sleep. She studies the drool down the side of Amber's mouth as it lands on the pillow. Deborah has never been able to sleep like this. With Dan it was in fits. He'd sprawl across the bed, forcing her to the edge. She wonders how Joe sleeps. Would he steal the covers? Some things she would no longer be willing to accommodate. Maybe it's best to sleep alone?

Deborah sits at the glass-top dining room table and sips from her mug. Amber stirs. The coffee tastes cheap and reliable.

Amber rises from the sofa. She rubs her eyes. "Can I have a cup?" she asks.

"The box is in the kitchen," Deborah replies. She's aware that's she's annoyed, but it's not with Amber. It's with herself. Again she has allowed circumstances to control her. She hears clanking in the kitchen. Amber appears with her coffee. "You're out of milk," Amber says.

And why am I the one to tiptoe? Deborah wonders.

"What happened to you in Malibu?" Deborah asks, feeling justified. After all Deborah was the one who saved her. Why couldn't she ask the obvious? Her own tearful conversations with the lawyers were overheard. And what did she really know about this stranger sleeping on her sofa?

"We were against titles and all they represent," says Amber, eyeing her empty coffee mug. "So we didn't call ourselves anything."

"I don't understand what you're talking about," Deborah says.

Amber tells her story. She'd grown up the youngest of a family of four in suburban Orange County. After graduating high school her parents paid for her to travel through Italy with a Catholic Church group. "But they were the real dangerous ones," said Amber. "It was about brainwashing and shutting down your spirit. Those nuns, they drove me crazy."

One afternoon, she took off. At a café in Venice she met three young Americans traveling on their own. "They invited me to join them and I basically never left. My parents were furious and demanded that I come home immediately or else they'd cut me off." Amber says making her choice seem easy. "Besides, I was never enough for them," she says about her family.

There was a guy of course. A goateed twenty-one year old named Matthew, with an impressive trust fund. He paid for Amber to continue on with them to Amsterdam, Paris and eventually a month-long spiritual retreat in India. By the time she returned to America it was the end of September. She missed what should have been her first month of college and wouldn't contact her parents.

Deborah would like another cup of coffee. She stands and remembers that Amber drank the last of the milk. She sits down. Amber continues. "Matthew said he needed my energy on his family land."

Deborah tries to imagine the Malibu Amber is describing, an area located in the canyons above her old house, ten acres of brush with an ocean view.

"The only way up was an old dirt road," Amber says. "We lived in yurts all over the property." Matthew was intent upon building a utopian society.

From her description, Deborah's certain that Amber had bought into his vision and gave up everything to live there. Are she and Amber so different after all?

"There were no rules. It was so different from where I grew up," says Amber.

"Tell me more about Matthew," Deborah says.

For the first time there is color in Amber's cheeks. "Matthew admired the Europeans," she says. "We'd sit around the campfires and listen to him speak between bong loads. "'America is lost and it's our duty to get it right,'" he'd say." 'We need to spread our knowledge to our generation and let them know that WalMart is our enemy. We need to disinfect ourselves. By living like this we return to society cleansed and work to make it right.' Deborah isn't sure who's talking anymore. Is it Amber or Matthew?

"So why did you leave?" she asks.

"Where does freedom end?" Amber says. "How can you talk about giving love and control it all at the same time?"

Did Amber leave or was she kicked out? Deborah knows that there is more to the story than Amber wants to share. There's more to her own story with Dan isn't there? The depression was a mask. There was the suicide plan and of course her own infidelity. These are the parts of her own story that she doesn't wish to share. Everyone self edits, don't they?

"I walked away from Matthew crying," Amber is saying. "I hiked down the narrow dirt trail towards the bottom of the canyon. I remember thinking that now it would be a life of my own. Then I bent down to tie my shoe and that's when the snake bit me. It was a sign."

"A sign of what?" Deborah asks nervously.

"Returning to the poisoned material world," Amber says.

Eleven

It was a few months before the wedding that Dan's parents came to Santa Monica for a speaking engagement at a local Marriage and Family Therapy conference. Dan had driven up from Orange County to meet them for lunch at The Ivy at the Shore. Deborah wasn't there. She had previous plans with a friend.

His parents stood up to hug him. They looked well, although unnaturally tan.

"You look great," Dan said and took the seat across from them at the patio table.

"We've taken up yoga," said his father, smiling and revealing his veneers.

Dan looked around the restaurant. People in casually expensive clothes leaned across tables and spoke in hushed tones, discussing new scripts or potential investors. Dan spoke to his parents in an imitative tone. In a softer than normal voice he described his new job at the law firm. He said things in short sentences: "It's a great firm. The hours are long. Excellent pay."

His parents nodded in encouragement and didn't ask many questions, for which he was thankful. Anyway, the law was a subject in which they were not well versed. They proudly proclaimed that they'd never been sued nor had they ever sued anyone. The only familiarity they might have shared with his career choice was their limited exposure to divorce lawyers, which for them represented failure.

They sipped cranberry passion fruit iced teas on the sun-lit patio and ordered overpriced salads for lunch. "The practice is very stable. I'm very confident with my decision," Dan said. He liked the sound of his voice. With every proclamation he slipped further away from being their son. In the distance he heard the squeals of children riding the Ferris wheel across the street on the pier. He listened to the roller coaster's wheels squeak as it climbed to the top of the metal track and the screams that followed. He imagined his soon-to-be future in the same way. Salads arrived on large white plates. They ate in carefully measured bites. A waiter brought fresh glasses of tea and removed the old ones collecting melted ice.

"Are you still anticipating a hundred guests?" asked his mother.

Dan nodded, his mouth full of grilled vegetables and lettuce.

"We feel so lucky that you and Deborah chose to have it at our house," his mother said.

"How are you feeling about the wedding?" asked his father rather loudly.

Dan looked up from his plate. "Deborah has everything handled on our end," he said and took another bite.

"I meant to say, how are you feeling about the marriage itself?" asked his father.

Dan looked around. To his relief their conversation was politely ignored. He looked back to his parents and wiped his mouth with the linen napkin. "Good," he said and placed it back on his lap.

"And Deborah? What is she expressing to you? Does she seem unusually nervous about the event?" asked his father.

"No. She's happy too," Dan said.

"You know that we think that she's a wonderful girl. Certainly smart and attractive," said his father.

"But, Daniel, you know that physical beauty does not last forever," said his mother. "And that there are things that bond a couple as lifetime partners. It takes a willingness to work hard at the marriage and to encourage each other's growth. The love between two people can grow deeper throughout the years if such intimacies exist."

Dan imagined his mother standing at a podium in a half full convention center and looked around the patio. He hoped the waiter would return soon. "Deborah's great," Dan said.

"We think so too," said his mother. "And as we always have, we give you unconditional love and complete emotional support. We extend this to you as a couple too."

Dan examined his silverware. It needed polishing.

"She does strike me as a bit aloof at times," said his father. "Does she offer you the intimacy that you need sexually?"

Dan took a long drink and raised a hand to signal the waiter.

"We just can't wait to deepen and explore our relationship with her," said his mother. Bits of lettuce were stuck in her teeth.

Dan nodded. The waiter brought the check. "I'm buying," said Dan.

"No, it's our treat," said his mother.

"Please. You've already done too much," Dan said. He pulled out his credit card and handed it to the waiter.

"He's asserting his new found sense of independence," said his father.

The waiter half smiled and walked away.

"We are so proud," said his mother. She stood up and walked around the table and hugged him. He noticed that people at the nearby tables were watching now.

"She was always so concerned about your introverted personality," his father said.

His mother went back to her seat and kissed his father on the lips. It was a long kiss. "My love for you grows stronger every day," she said to his father.

The waiter retuned with the bill and Dan quickly signed it. "Let's go," he said and pocketed his credit card and receipt. He would write it off as a business lunch. They stood up and walked through the crowded patio. The valet brought their cars and after more hugging Dan sped home.

Twelve

She lives in a ghost town. A lone tumbleweed rolls across the empty street. Deborah takes Amber's arm and guides her along. "Keep your head down," she says. She knows that all of the new development is happening in the east: Indian Wells, La Quinta, Indio and even The Salton Sea. Palm Springs is left to rot, she thinks, Manifest Destiny.

Deborah opens the door of the ice cream shop; she's greeted by air conditioning and a heavily pierced employee who nods begrudgingly. Amber rushes to the counter to order and Deborah pays the girl for the cone and they sit at a small metal table at the rear.

"I'd kill for you," Amber says. Strawberry ice cream drips from the corner of her mouth.

Deborah picks up the rough white napkin and dabs Amber's chin. "Finish your cone," she says.

Amber extends the ice cream to Deborah. "Wanna lick?"

Deborah nods. More than the taste, she enjoys the feeling of the ice cream against her dry cracked lips. The desert has left her dehydrated.

"But Dan wants to take everything," Amber says. Her pupils look wild under the glare of the florescent lighting.

Deborah knows that she's overheard her conversations with the lawyer. They live in a small place with thin walls. "No, not everything," Deborah says. She's watching the girl behind the counter write on her hand with a ballpoint pen. Air conditioning blasts down from an overhead vent and Deborah shivers. "There is his gun in Malibu," Deborah hears herself saying the words and immediately regrets it. She doesn't even know what she means or why she's said it.

Amber smiles. Her teeth are pink.

Deborah stands. The metal chair squeals as she pushes away from the table, "I'll be back," she says.

She sits on the toilet and reads the scribbled writing etched onto the back of the bathroom door. "Sydney is a slut." "You are a dirty whore." "Why are you so lame to write on walls." Signs of angry women. She spoke of Dan's gun out of anger. Why would she hint about it to Amber? Even if he acts like a jerk, she'd certainly she'd never want anything bad to happen to Dan. Would she? Where has her anger lead her?

Thirteen

Deborah looks out of the living room window. It is night. Rain is falling on the desert floor. Television had marked their daylight hours.

"Can't you see what's happening?" Amber asks and presses her face against the glass.

"I see rain," replies Deborah. She sits on the sofa and crosses her long legs elegantly.

"The desert is alive. It's drinking it in," Amber says. She puts her palms against the glass and traces the rain.

"Watch out, you'll leave marks," says Deborah.

"Exactly," Amber replies, "something to remember me by. Come on." She turns from the window.

Deborah watches her with curiosity. It was what made her chase a leaf down the street as a little girl. And it was what the Captain repeatedly told her would get her into trouble later on. She never did, though. At least not yet.

Deborah follows Amber outside. "Keep your clothes on," she says.

Amber flashes a wicked grin. She heads toward the desert, seemingly oblivious to the rain that had previously captivated her. "Follow me," she says, skipping ahead. Deborah walks behind her, down the driveway and into the desert. It's a different place at night. The moon is full.

Amber is singing, "He bumped his head and couldn't get up in the morning."

"Slow down," Deborah says, thinking of rattlesnakes and coyotes.

Amber continues undisturbed. She's kicking up the barely moistened sand. Deborah watches her hair bounce and glow in the moonlight. She envies her youthfulness. "Amber," Deborah calls out but she's ignored. Time is not present here. She wonders if she is really here at all or if all of this is just a dream, but she knows it's not.

In the distance is a cluster of smoke trees. Their long skinny branches spread out like fingers. Deborah feels frightened as she watches Amber disappear among them. She suddenly feels lost. She looks back towards her condominium and sees it as just a small speck. She realizes how far she has gone. Her marriage is over and she's living in the desert. How has it come to this?

She wants to turn back but not without Amber. "Amber," Deborah calls out and reluctantly enters the smoke trees. Someone could get hurt out here, she thinks as she sees an old mattress and the rusted frame of a car. In the distance she hears thumping. She realizes that it's a bass line, steadily repeated. She pushes her way out of the smoke trees and sees flashing multicolored lights.

Amber is spinning. Her golden hair flying. "Deborah!" she cries out, "I'm flying!"

Deborah thinks of her mother this way. She's five years old and lying back in the middle of the merry go round at the park. The sun is playing a game of hide and seek behind the puffy white clouds. Deborah is certain that it's her mother spinning her. She tries to remember the sound of her mother's laughter. The merry go round stops and Deborah feels hit by a wave of nausea. She stands and throws up on her new white Buster Brown sandals.

Amber is running ahead towards the circle of pickup trucks parked in the distance. The base of the mountain is ignited in color and sound.

Aimless dancers are moving on the wet sand to the pulsating beats. They're wearing baggy overalls and sucking on glow stick pacifiers. Amber is in the crowd.

"Amber," Deborah calls, but her voice is lost in the music. What if I can't find her, she thinks and begins to panic. She looks around frantically and there is the golden blond hair. In the middle of the commotion Amber is kissing a blond Rastafarian.

Suddenly two white spotlights illuminate the crowd. The sheriffs arrive in SUVs. As quickly as the party appeared it is now dispersing. Trucks are racing out in all directions. Ravers jump into cab beds and escape. Dust is rising from the desert floor.

Deborah moves with the fleeing crowd. She has no other choice as she's being pushed ahead. She feels like she's one of them now. This is her initiation. She runs toward the smoke trees, thinking she can hide there. I can't go back without her, she realizes. She hardly recognizes herself.

In the middle of the trees, Amber is sitting on a mattress. Deborah tries not to imagine what has taken place there. "Get up," she says, "let's get out of here."

Amber is laughing like this is a game. "Run as fast as you can," Amber sings.

Deborah pulls her up and soon they're running across the moonlit desert holding hands. Last week she was dining at Nobu with Dan and now she is fleeing from the police. No one is left to bail her out.

The condominiums are illuminated in the distance. The police are nowhere in sight. As the rain gently falls they skip the rest of the way home.

Fourteen

The blond Rastafarian and two skinheads are standing next to a dirty Expedition under the carport. Deborah wishes that she could turn and walk away. But it's too late.

"Want to party at Monty's ranch?" the Rastafarian is asking.

Deborah is annoyed by their presumptions.

"We're going home now," Deborah replies. It's starting to rain harder and Deborah wants to get inside. Amber places her hands on her hips and pushes them out to the side. Is this what flirting looks like now? Deborah wonders. She is feeling too old for this game. "Come on Amber," she says and walks towards the condo. She can feel their stares penetrating her from behind. She feels violated.

"You're not my mother," Amber says.

Deborah turns to face her as the words slap against her face. She walks away. She can hear them laughing. She reaches her front door and hears the squeal of tires. She imagines the Expedition racing down the driveway. Deborah runs towards them, but it's too late. Amber has left.

It's pouring rain. Deborah's hair is wet. She stands motionless by the side of the driveway. She's not sure what she would have done differently.

Fifteen

She lies awake in bed waiting for Amber to return. Will she knock on the front door or just barge right in? Will she bring one or all three men with her? Deborah is spinning in a web of possibilities, all of which leave her feeling uneasy and insecure. She pictures Amber in a back bedroom somewhere getting gangbanged and enjoying it. She pictures Amber leading a drinking competition with a room full of men. But mostly she pictures Amber waking up on her sofa.

She is shocked when morning finally comes and Amber hasn't returned.

Besides, there are questions. Things Deborah thought she'd ask Amber at a better time. Why did you attempt suicide? Wasn't there anyone else that you could have gone to? It seems ridiculous not to have turned to Amber during a commercial and asked. Maybe it was because they were the same questions that she wanted to avoid for herself.

Deborah gets out of bed and walks into the kitchen. She runs the facet water into the tall glass and takes a drink. She puts the glass down on the counter and walks out the front door. She shakes her head as she looks outside for a sign of Amber's return. An elderly man using a walker is opening the pool gate.

"Good day, young lady," the man at the gate calls to her.

She smiles. "Good morning," she says.

Sixteen

Dan returns to work on Monday morning. He had spent the weekend cleaning the house, calling in a favor from the city's top divorce attorney and even washing his own car. He also decided to train for a marathon and began with a nine mile run along the coast. He's sore but finally able to concentrate on work.

After the sunset, Dan gets into his car for home. On PCH he finds himself in bumper-to-bumper traffic. He sees red brake lights. He can't believe that Deborah would choose to leave their Malibu lifestyle.

The commute takes an hour but he finally turns up the narrow road leading to his house. *My house.* He pauses in consideration. When he let himself in, the spotless house awaits him. He doesn't need Rosa or anyone else, he thinks. He pours himself a drink. The vodka burns its way down his throat and into the pit of his empty stomach. He walks into the kitchen, loosens his tie and opens a cabinet. First just the one but soon all the rest. He goes into the dining room and opens the leaves of the large buffet table. Unsatisfied, he continues into the den, the office and all of the bathrooms. In each room he grows increasingly discontent. He cannot find any trace of Deborah in this entire house. He would have been satisfied to find a small jar of her rose-scented hand lotion or a bobby pin. There is nowhere left to look. A modern-style house is not designed to hold memories.

Dan walks into the closed room that would have been the nursery. It sits empty now, except for a pastel pink dresser. He pulls open drawers and slams them shut. They're also empty. He sits down on the carpet and looks out of the large picture window. He hasn't thought much of the baby since the day that she was cremated. Once the flowers stopped arriving at the house, he put the experience behind him. When light from the full moon shines down upon him, he knows that all traces of Deborah are gone. A book, an old unframed photograph, even an old grocery list: things that she would have inadvertently left behind in a hasty decision to leave him. But he knows now that these things, these bits of her, must have disappeared months ago. Slowly piece-by-piece she had left this house long before she announced to him that she wanted a divorce. Most likely starting the afternoon that she returned home alone from the hospital. At the time, his business meeting had seemed so important.

Dan walks across the room into the moonlight. For the first time since she left, he cries.

Seventeen

It's been three days since Amber left and what Deborah wants now is Joe. The heat of his skin masking her coldness. Despite everything, she hopes that Amber will return. Joe would understand this because he was there that day.

Dan had called in the middle of the night. She got out of bed and answered the living room phone hoping it would've been someone else. He began by saying that he was sorry for trying to block her access to their joint accounts and that he would respect her decision for a quick divorce if she was sure that it was indeed over.

She had said it was and that it had been for what felt like a long time now.

He urged her to reconsider.

She wasn't certain that she was awake until she stumbled in the dark and nearly fell over the coffee table on the way back to her bedroom. He sounded drunk. Maybe things would be different in the morning. But so far she hadn't heard back from him or any of his lawyers.

She thinks that maybe once her divorce is settled and Joe is sober, they will find a vacant lot. It will be in the desert and will have a water tower. No one else will understand its potential so they can buy it for almost nothing. Joe will open his scuba school. She will be his first student. On her Bora Bora honeymoon with Dan she had tried but failed. He paid the locals to allow her to dive without certification. She panicked, felt sure the ocean would swallow her. But this time will be different. Joe will gently slip her mask on and guide her slowly into the tank. They will hold hands on their descent. It will be effortless.

Deborah sits on the living room safe and reaches for the phone. She dials information before she can talk herself out of it.

She is connected to a Julie Cohen in the 818 area code. On the second ring a groggy sounding man answers the telephone.

"May I speak to Joe please?" she asks, bracing herself to hear his voice.

"Don't ever call this number again," the man says and hangs up on her.

She feels like she is drowning. She walks across the living room and opens the small hall closet. She stands on her tiptoes to reach the top shelf. She grabs the camera bag and pulls it down. It falls into her arms. She grabs her keys from the kitchen table and walks outside. The sunlight blinds her for a moment.

She walks across the grass, past the pool and into the open desert where she ran with Amber. She sets the bag down on the hot sand and pulls out the camera.

The thick nylon strap feels heavy around Deborah's neck. She has forgotten its weight. The Captain said her interest in photography was a waste of time and money.

She pauses and lifts the camera to her eye. What can she find out here? Through the viewfinder she scans the width of the desert, taking in the cacti. She is looking for something else. She hopes to spot Amber through the lens in the distance, her snow-like complexion contrasting the heat of the desert landscape. Maybe she will find her again. Any of the three of them will make a good subject. If not Amber then her lost mother or dead daughter. The three will be standing far off in a glittering mirage. She will drink them in like water. She is excessively thirsty now. And then she catches sight of life. To her right a roadrunner dashes across the sand. She tracks it with her lens, anxious to follow something living. It pauses by a bush and turns its neck in precise clocklike motions.

Deborah kneels and photographs the bird until the wind causes it to scurry off across the desert. Deborah stands and lowers the camera. She walks past the broken bits of tumbleweeds back towards her home.

Eighteen

She thinks of her body like a hermit crab's shell. A part of her has moved out leaving room for something else. Yesterday, on the phone, Deborah's lawyer advised her to get a job.

"Take whatever work you can find," he said. "Even something low paying for now. It'll make you look sympathetic."

She thought that in any case it would help to be busy. She'd been unemployed for too long.

Deborah drives down Palm Canyon Boulevard. There's a shop with a painted turquoise exterior. She pulls the Range Rover over and parks at the nearest curb. A "Help Wanted" sign caught her attention in the store window.

She gets out of the car. The large sign in peach lettering over the front door reads, THE DATE SHACK. The cash stuffed in her front pocket still feels like Dan's. She pushes open the glass door. Inside she's greeted by acne faced boy. He's wearing tan pants and a white button down shirt. His nametag reads, "HI! I am David, Do You Want A Date?"

No, she immediately thinks.

"I'm Deborah. I'm looking for a job," she says.

"My sister went to the bank. She'll be back in six minutes. Deborah," he says and studies her seriously. His eyes are black and intense. "Do you love dates? I mean really love them?"

Deborah nods and shrugs at the same time.

"I'll give you an autograph," he says.

"I don't follow," she says.

David points to the "Date Wall of Fame". There's a photograph of someone dressed as a giant date.

"Can you keep a secret?" he whispers and leans towards her.

She nods, unsure if she should walk out.

"That's my alter ego Medjool the Great. You can be Lois Lane," he says raising his eyebrows.

David removes a Styrofoam tray from behind the counter. It's full of chopped up little pieces of dates. "These originally came from Morocco. They're soft, luscious, sweet in taste, perfect in texture and ship well. Our best seller. Would you like a sample?" He hands Deborah a yellow plastic toothpick that looks like a tiny sword.

The shop door opens and a young woman walks in. Her face is long and angular. She looks concerned.

"And presenting the next Queen of Iran, my sister, Natalya," says David, bowing while carefully balancing the fruit. "This is Deborah and she wants a job."

"You're going to run her out of the shop," says Natalya.

Deborah chews. He's right, she thinks. The date is sweet.

Natalya extends a slim dark hand to Deborah. "I'm sorry about him."

Deborah smiles. "I'm just not interested in wearing a costume."

Natalya's face softens. "I totally get it," she says. "We just need a part time cashier."

The next day, she starts her new job. She assures herself that it's only temporary. And on her days off, Deborah uses her camera and looks for animals with the intensity that she realizes she should have used to locate her mother. Surely she could have stashed some cash and hired a private investigator. When her father was still alive her excuse had been that she didn't want to disrespect him. But now that he's dead, what's stopping her?

She knows by now that it's easiest to find the animals at night. Reasonable, she thinks, since most of them are nocturnal. And if she had listened more closely to her father's few descriptions then she'd have known that her mother would be nocturnal too. Maybe that's the real reason Deborah never looks for her. She is afraid of what she might find.

The moon is full and the sand white. Deborah is no longer scared. Amber had given her this much, she thinks, remembering the rave in the desert. She waits quietly outside of the smoke trees. In the desert, you can never be sure of what you might find. She knows this now, since she has finally found a life that she might want to call her own. She has her photography and a job. If she looks long enough she's sure that she'll discover the rest of what she wants but for now she waits patiently. The first sign of life will soon emerge. To most people this place looks like nothingness, but she knows better now. It's full of life. It's just that this life has adapted itself to a highly developed mode of survival. She hopes that her photographs will tell her story.

Nineteen

The extreme heat reminds her of the fog rolling in at the beach in Malibu. It covers everything. At work, Natalya complains that there aren't any customers. She says tomorrow she'll have to cut back hours. Deborah understands. Besides, she wants to spend more time working on her photography. She watches Natalya who's sitting behind the counter reading People magazine. The cover is filled with girls in bikinis. "Malibu Movie Star Summer", it reads. It's the beach across the street from her former house.

David emerges from the rear of the store dressed up as a date.

"What're you doing? You'll drop dead from a heat stroke!" Natalya says. She drops her magazine dramatically for effect on the countertop.

"I'll never be stopped by the weather, and stop calling me David," he says. He salutes her and walks outside. The heat pours into the store.

"He's a fucking nut," Natalya says.

"No, he's a fucking date," Deborah replies.

Natalya smiles, turns the page of her magazine and adds, "Actually, a date is a nut."

"I think the heat has gotten to our heads," Deborah says.

"I'd take a beach house in Malibu right now," Natalya says. "Look at these people," she says, flashing the magazine at Deborah.

"I used to live there," Deborah says. "It all looks better on film than in real life."

Natalya looks intrigued and sets her magazine down. Deborah tells her about her life with Dan. It feels good to share her version of the story. Saying everything out loud is therapeutic. It's too bad that she and Dan never gave therapy a try.

"Now I won't be so envious of those beach girls this summer," Natalya says and puts her magazine under the counter. "And, the good news here is if you make it through your first summer you'll be elevated to the status of a real local."

Was she ever a true Malibu local?

Twenty

Nothing looks like it did last night. The white covers on his bed look slightly yellowed. Light pours into the room through the already open curtains. Dan steps over a pile of dirty clothes. Dust is rising from the floor. There's a pounding upstairs. It was this noise that woke him. He walks into the closet and puts on his robe. He walks upstairs and hears the banging on the front door. He walks faster across the cold marble floor.

"Don't cry," he told his mother last night over the phone after finally confiding to his parents about the divorce. "There's nothing that you could have done," he reassured her.

"But that's what we're here for," she'd said.

"No it's not," he said and it felt good, so he continued. "There were things that she and I needed to share alone. Things were avoided until they forced us apart."

And gratefully, his mother left it at that.

The first thing that irritates Dan is that this strange guy standing in his doorway chooses to put his cigarette out on the doorstep, oblivious to the fact that he had woken Dan and that he was also littering. Of course Dan was annoyed from the onset, with the doorbell and the pounding waking him from his first night of uninterrupted sleep since she left. But the second annoyance is the man's bright red t-shirt with the lightning bolt ironed across the chest.

"Nice shirt," Dan says. He remembers being young and riding his Big Wheel in Superhero Underoos. Without meaning to, he smiles.

"Sorry to wake you," says the man. The wind blows hot and strong. The man stuffs his hands into his shorts pockets and looks down.

Dan hopes he'll decide to pick up his cigarette butt. Instead, the wind does the job and carries it away from the house. Regretfully, Dan watches it blow towards the canyons. He runs his hand through his disheveled hair and pulls the tie of his robe tighter. "What's up?" Dan asks, assuming that this is how he should speak to someone his own age who looks like this.

"I'm Joe," says the man in a way that expects a gesture of recognition.

Dan shrugs. "What can I do for you," he says.

"I'm looking for Deb," Joe says.

Maybe it's the way that he says Deb. Or maybe it's the air of casual arrogance that surrounds him, but in any case Dan decides that he dislikes this Joe. Dan narrows his eyes, wondering what kind of association would justify this strange man calling his wife by a nickname. "She's not here," he says.

"Will she be back?" Joe says.

Dan sees that Joe's eyes are bloodshot, like a surfer or a stoner. Maybe both. "I don't think so," he says and steps back to shut the door.

Joe, somehow anticipating this, puts his hand up to stop it from closing. "Listen, man, I think she's in trouble,"

Dan puts his hands into his robe pockets and clenches them into fists. "Why are you telling me this?" he says.

The neighbor across the street is waving hello and getting into her car. Dan nods in her direction. Joe turns to look. Now would be the time to knock him in the head. Otherwise, Dan realizes, he might not stand a chance against him. Joe is taller and broader and looks like he hasn't spent the last fifteen years of his life anchored to a desk. The neighbor smiles and waves as she drives away.

"Wasn't that chick on All My Children?" Joe asks.

"I wouldn't know. I don't watch daytime TV," Dan says.

"Anyway, look, I helped Deb get this crazy chick to an Urgent Care. I was staying at Horizons down the street. But I'm in a much better rehab now."

"Congratulations," Dan says.

"Thanks," says Joe, oblivious to the sarcasm, "This friend of mine there, he's a major producer. Anyway he tells me he decided to cough up the sixty grand to enter the program after he partied with this crazy chick at his house on Broad Beach. The last night she was there she tied him up and robbed him."

"What does this have to do with my wife?" Dan asks.

"This girl was telling everyone that a rattlesnake in Malibu Canyon bit her. It was this crazy girl that Deb and I helped."

Dan could barely recall the conversation about it. He leans his head toward his shoulder and cracks his neck.

"Deb was really concerned about this girl," Joe says. "It was very sweet. You know how she visited her at the hospital and everything."

"Sure," Dan lied.

"Some nurse at the hospital gave her Deb's address in the desert to send her a thank you note."

"So what's the problem?" asks Dan.

"She told my buddy that she was going to deliver it to her in person."

Dan cracks his neck. Maybe there was someone else in the condo when he called her. It was hard to tell because Deborah always hung up the phone so fast.

"If that chick finds your wife then she could be in danger," Joe says.

"If you knew she's in the desert, why come here looking for her?" Dan asks.

The wind blew.

"I never thought that she'd really leave Malibu," Joe says. "It's beautiful here. Besides, this rehab that I'm in, I can't just take off. But I had to warn her."

"How brave of you," Dan says. He thinks about the gun in his closet.

"Thanks. Actually, that producer is getting me a gig as a stunt man in this ocean adventure picture that he's going to start working on in a few months. We'll be shooting in the Caribbean." Joe takes out a cigarette and lights it.

"Sounds like a great opportunity," Dan says. "Is that your secret, Joe? You just move from one easy opportunity to the next?"

Joe turns and exhales his smoke to the side. "Hey listen, I walked three miles to get here. You don't have to be an asshole."

"You really outdid yourself," Dan says. "And by the way, her name is Deborah." He steps back slams the door.

That scumbag fucked my wife, he thinks. Dan walks quickly across the house and downstairs. He can feel his heart racing. In his closet he throws on clothes. Did she let him into their house? He reaches the staircase and then turns, walks back into his closet, opens his underwear drawer and gets out his bullets and gun. It feels heavy in his hand. He grabs a box of bullets and his coat.

Twenty-One

Traffic clears after LA. Dan turns on the radio. FM, AM, CD, IPod. He turns them off. Nothing satisfies him. He heard his parents say this through the walls, in the darkness of his bedroom when he was eleven. It's true. Only the sound of her voice begging for his forgiveness will appease him.

Dan looks at the passenger seat, empty except for his jacket and the loaded gun. He sits up straight. His back hurts. He imagines what she will say. Will she lie about sleeping with Joe? Then she'll be a whore and a liar, he decides.

The freeway is empty. He accelerates to a hundred. Strip malls and outlet shops pass on either side of the car. He is not distracted. The past years have proved to be too full of distractions. Dan looks straight ahead with forced determination. This is the drive that he has always possessed. He should be in the desert in an hour. If he goes faster, it could be even quicker. What will he say when he first sees her? He remembers the gun. What if he gets pulled over? A fear rises within him. He's not sure whom he's afraid of; the police, Deborah or himself. He isn't sure what he's doing.

He eases his foot off the gas pedal and slows down to eighty. He will still make good time. He rolls down the window. The air is hot on his unshaven face. He narrows his eyes to focus on the road ahead. He will not be distracted.

Twenty-Two

Deborah heard the muffled apology in her sleep. She opened her eyes slowly. Amber was kneeling at her bedside. The golden mane had transformed into a tangled mess. Deborah reached out to smooth it. She wanted to say, all is forgiven but cold metal tightened around her wrist. She watched herself being handcuffed to the brass bedpost. "What are you doing," she said. She was now awake.

"Didn't want to freak you out but I had a sudden urge to tie you up," said Amber, her eyes filled with madness.

Deborah pulled against the bed. She was unable to get away.

Amber left the bedroom and Deborah called after her. She was ignored. Left to rot. Again she pulled against the bedpost. The metals rattled against one another. Her body was shaking.

"They're all against me," Amber said from the other room. Drawers opened and shut. "Everyone but you, Deborah. You were my only friend."

Deborah was unable to speak. She was sweating from fighting against herself. She was able to stand by the side of her bed, but there was no phone in this room. No one would call her in the middle of the night. She had never been that kind of friend. Although she now hopes that if she escapes she may someday be. She sees now that what she had with Amber was obviously not friendship. It was just another distraction.

"And everything I'm taking is for your own good," called Amber from the next room. "Besides, it was paid for with his money anyway. This will be your freedom."

Sure, Deborah thinks as she pulled on her handcuffs. She hears glass shattering. Amber is crazy.

"Our society is corrupted. Look at what we've done to our planet in the name of consumerism," Amber says in a voice that Deborah doesn't recognize.

Deborah's head falls back on the pillow. She hears the front door open and close. She braces herself for whatever will come next.

Amber has gone. Deborah's insides twist and turn wanting to escape in one moment and trying to accept the fact that she created this situation in the next. She has no one else to blame. She is thrashing on her bed like a shark brought to land. She screams and hopes that her voice will carry through the thin walls. But who will hear her? Her old suicide plan strikes her as especially absurd now. She laughs and lets her head fall back on the pillow. The memory of marching into the canyon with Dan's gun seems comical now.

She pulls against the bedposts. She wants to live. From somewhere outside of her body, she hears herself calling for help. She does this for hours. During this time she studies her black and white photographs lining the bedroom walls. They document life in the desert. After awhile she realizes that they actually document her life here. Proof of her ability to survive and build an independent existence. A life existing contrary to appearances: A lone coyote with hungry eyes, the cautious roadrunner, and a snake slithering to safety.

Now she recalls the snake in Malibu. It bit Amber. She'd found Amber in the road. The snake had brought them together. The snake drew her closer to Joe because she thought she needed him to get Amber to Urgent Care. The snake led her back to the place where she'd miscarried so she'd face the effect on her and what was left of her marriage.

The bite had transformed the direction of her life. In fact, it possibly saved her. Now she wants freedom from this physical restraint. The handcuffs. She's suddenly confident that she can overcome the rest. The emotional, spiritual and mental help that she needs is available. In fact it's always been. She was never willing to look at all that was available to her. Now things have become clearer. She knows what she wants and what she doesn't. Her life has come into focus. Her wrists ache from the metal handcuffs, but she won't stop her fight until she is free.

Twenty-Three

He walks along the uncomfortably familiar path. It's hot. Each step he takes is faster than the next, until he's almost running to her door. He's angry with himself for doing exactly what he swore he would not. Especially after all that had happened but maybe now because of that.

The responsibility he feels for her bears down upon him like a weight in his chest. It's the same feeling that has plagued him ever since she left. Late nights, awake and alone in bed, trying to figure out who actually left first. On the day that their daughter died was there really nothing that he could offer Deborah? Dan thought back then that it was space that she needed. It certainly was what he constantly craved. And now, what did Deborah need? Was it a man like Joe? He wipes a trail of sweat from his forehead. He hears what sounds likes a scream. He tells himself that it could be a cat in heat. That would be ironic and he thinks of Deborah and Joe in his bed.

His hands shakes as he digs inside his jacket pocket for the keys but instead feels his gun. Again he hears the sound. It is coming from inside. The condominium key is in his other pocket. He takes it out. Despite everything, he feels anxious to be the one to rescue her. So many times he has failed her. He realizes that now. It's what has kept him awake at night. The guilt and regret of things left unsaid. Moments when he should have been there and maybe he was physically but he never reached out and offered her what was inside of himself. But what is that? Maybe his car, job and house are all that he has?

Dan opens the door. There has to be more. He walks into the living room. A lamp is knocked over, the television set is gone and all the cabinets have been left open. It looks like a TV show that he'd avoid watching because it would seem cliché. But here he finds himself standing in the middle of it all. He walks towards the bedroom door. He holds onto the gun, unsure if he'll be able to use it. He opens the door and finds Deborah handcuffed to the bed. Her eyes are wide with fright.

"Get the hell out of here," Deborah says.

He's taken aback but not altogether surprised. "Is she still here?" he asks in a quiet voice.

Deborah shakes her head and pulls against the bedpost. "I said get out!" she yells. She does not want him to find her like this. After all, this is not who she had become. She had a job and for the first time, in a decade, a direction. Just last week she signed up for a photography class. It wasn't supposed to be like this. If anyone were to rescue her, then let it have been Joe.

He goes to the kitchen and brings her a glass of water. He extends it to her. She slides her body up the bed and manages to sit up a bit. He holds it to her mouth. Her lips are chapped. He sees the fine lines around her mouth and wants to kiss her but can't. She seems reluctant to take a sip from the glass. "Please, Deborah," he says.

Her eyes meet his. His brow is furrowed. She's overcome by thirst and drinks from the glass. It feels cool against her mouth. Soon she finishes it.

"I'm calling the police now," he says.

After speaking to the police he returns to the bedroom. Deborah is lying on her back, staring at the ceiling. He'd ask if she was okay but he knows that she's not. And so he says the truth. "I'm sorry."

"How did you know to come?" she asks.

"Joe," he says. The name falls between them like a wall. He looks down at the shaggy carpeted floor.

"Why isn't he here, then?" she asks.

He looks up and meets her eyes. They look hopeful. He doesn't want to disappoint her but still he says, "He's back in rehab."

She nods. "But he came up to the house to warn me, to help you," says Dan. He can't believe that he finds himself defending this Joe. This stranger who put his cigarette out on his front porch and left it there to let the wind carry it away.

"I slept with him," Deborah says. Her eyes offer him a challenge.

"I figured that," Dan says.

He hears sirens.

She looks at him. "What you and I had ended a long time ago."

"Was it always like this?" Dan asks.

Deborah pulls on the bedposts and groans. Her wrists are red. She rolls her head. Long black hair falls into her eyes.

He is still attracted to her. It's like seeing her for the first time. Dan looks up at the popcorn ceiling. It should be removed.

"It was just like this," Deborah says and pulls on the handcuffs. The sirens are loud. "It was you needing to help me. Term papers. Directions. Even in bed. Like I was some injured creature that you rescued and I followed thinking it was true."

"Maybe I didn't know what to give you then. But now," Dan says looking at her again.

"The funny part is," Deborah says looking at him, "in the end, when that was the truth and I did need you, you weren't there. Why did you go back to work after the miscarriage? Why was that the priority? Fuck you, Dan. And fuck me for not knowing better," she says.

Dan moves to the foot of her bed and sits. He doesn't know where to start. He can't blame his parents, God or her. He is the only one left. He looks at the carpet.

"I want you to leave when they get here," she says.

"I'm not sure that I can," he says. There are things that he can offer her now that he couldn't before. He could be a friend. He knows this now.

"When it's time, I want you to go. Things have happened which you can't understand," she says. She thinks of her sadness and guilt about losing their child. How she has isolated herself in order to survive.

"I think I can understand now," he says.

She knows that she shares the blame. Her instincts were created when her own mother left. But this is not that time.

There's a pounding on the door.

Dan gets up.

"It's best you leave," she says, avoiding his eyes. She can barely hear her own thoughts. Amber stole the last of her naivete but in doing so also gave her this gift. She is finally thankful to be alive. A heartbeat inside her chest, a thirst quenched by water, and time still left.

Dan walks out to let the police in.

Twenty-Four

In the end, Dan did leave. Finally he listened. The police left her yellow papers, stiff business cards and a Xeroxed copy of resources to help with post-traumatic stress syndrome. Standing in her doorway, she ushered them out and counted, one, two, three police officers out her front door. She clutched the copied paperwork and promised to call if she needed help. This time, she told the truth. She closed the door and turned to face the mess in her condo.

Soon after, she calls Natalya, who shows up half an hour later carrying a platter of unfamiliar-looking food. Following Natalya into the condo is David dressed up as Medjool the Date.

"I tried to stop him from putting on the costume. But he insisted. He said that it would cheer you up," Natalya says.

Deborah follows her into the kitchen while David dances around the living room. The food smells horrible.

"I'm happy for the help," Deborah says.

"Unbelievable," Natalia says. "She must be totally insane."

"It appears that way," Deborah says.

She forces herself to eat their dinner. David sets the giant date head in the middle of the living room and emerges red faced and sweaty from underneath the costume. They talk about what happened. Deborah feels good to have people around. After dinner they set out to clean the rest of the mess. Deborah allows them to help push the sofa back into place and pick up papers. David vacuums dirt spilled from a potted plant. More than ever, Deborah is grateful for their friendship.

"Are you going to stay here?" Natalya asks, holding a bottle of Windex and a paper towel.

"I'm not sure," says Deborah. "I don't have a plan."

The crime scene only took a few hours to clean. "I'm fine to sleep here," Deborah says as her friends turn to leave. She promises that she'll call if she changes her mind.

She doesn't call.

In the morning she finds that she slept though the night. She will start the rebuilding process again. It'll be different this time. She thinks of the photography class, which starts next week, and the people that she'll meet there. She looks forward to learning more about her craft and continuing her work in the desert. She'll document the life that thrives in the midst of what appears to be only nothingness.

Twenty-Five

Dan is in a crowd ready to begin the Malibu 10k race. Men and women stretch their muscular legs. Everyone is tan. The waves are crashing. He feels confident that he will place among the top of his age division. He trained hard all month. Weekdays he left work early to run. Weekends he ran some more.

His heart pounds in anticipation of the starting gun. In his mind he visualizes himself crossing the finish line. First place. He bends down and double-knots his shoelaces. When he stands he sees a familiar face. He catches the man's eye and smiles. It's Weinstein from law school. He graduated first in their class. Dan excuses his way through the racers.

"It's been too long," Dan says, reaching his old friend.

Alex Weinstein smiles and pats Dan on the back. Alex still looks like he did in college: wavy brown hair, long thin legs. "Great to see you, Dan," he says.

"I thought you were with Eisenberg, Eisenberg and Ellis in New York. Are you here on vacation?" Dan asks.

"I left four years ago. Sarah and I wanted to be closer to our family here. We have two kids now. Twin five year-old girls. Rebecca and Rachel," Alex says.

Dan smiles. "Congratulation," he says. "What firm are you with? I'm surprised that I haven't heard about you."

"You wouldn't have. I'm working in the Valley as a public defender," Alex says.

A celebrity announcer welcomes the race participants over the PA.

"I'll bring you in to meet my partners and we'll get you a position," Dan says.

The crowd is anxious to begin.

"I love what I'm doing," Alex says. "I've never been happier. I have more time for my family and I'm making a difference."

"So maybe I should talk to you about a job," Dan says and shrugs.

Alex raises his eyebrows. "The pay sucks," he says.

"I'm serious," Dan says.

"We certainly need lawyers like you," Alex says.

The gun goes off. The crowd dashes forward and swerves to avoid the two men in their way. Dan remembers giving his gun away to the policeman outside of Deborah's condo after she'd been released from the handcuffs. He was glad that he no longer owned a firearm. It had been a stupid decision to ever keep one in their house. And what if they had children?

"It's been a bad year," Dan says. "I'm ready for a change." A woman runner bumps into him as she tries to make her way around. "Sorry," he calls to her. She doesn't look back.

"Meet me at the finish line. You can see Sarah and our kids. We'd love to see Deborah," Alex says as runners continue to maneuver around them.

"She left me," Dan says.

"I'm sorry," Alex says. He places a hand on Dan's shoulder.

"Me too," Dan says. "I'm serious about change."

Alex smiles. "Then I'll see you at the finish line," he says and runs away.

Dan takes a breath. The ocean smells good. He stretches his arms overhead and bends side to side. Suddenly the race seems unimportant. Ridiculous even. He's not even sure why he entered. He's the last racer to begin. He starts off slow. He can feel his breath move through his body. The waves crash along the shore. The smell of the ocean is strong. He breathes in deeply through his nose and exhales. He remembers Deborah. They were living in Orange County. It was a weekend afternoon, a few years after the wedding. Those years are hard to number. Work was blinding.

Deborah was in the backyard on her hands and knees. She was planting colorful flowers around the border of the small grass lawn. It was a hot day.

"Why are you wasting your time? We don't own the place," he'd said and took a sip of bottled water. He stood in the opening of the sliding door and watched her work.

She turned to him. Sweat dripped from her forehead. "But we live here," she said.

At the time, he'd never considered those years in Orange County as anything more than temporary. It had been a stepping stone, a means to an end. For what? He wonders and feels ashamed.

Ahead of him now, in the distance, he sees the pack of runners headed towards the hills. He can't convince himself to speed up. Keeping his slow pace, he remembers. Deborah had dragged him to a flea market one Sunday afternoon to buy furniture for the rental house. He didn't want to be there. He had important work to do.

She'd smiled and pointed at old bookcases. "This one would be nice in the living room," she said.

He shrugged. It didn't matter to him. Living in Orange County wasn't what he wanted. But what did she want? He has questions that he'd like to ask her now. Things he should have asked years ago. How did she spend the evenings waiting for him to come home? What books did she read and what did she think of what they tried to say? Did she enjoy her job? When they moved to Malibu where did she go during the day? And the baby, when she died how did it make her feel? Obviously sad, he'd seen her tears. But there was more that he needed to say to her. He should have taken time away from work. They should have held hands and taken long walks on the beach. He should have told her how he was feeling too. That it broke his heart and he didn't have the words to explain how he felt. He didn't want to overwhelm her emotionally the way that his parents always overwhelmed him. But to just ignore it and pretend that it never happened. That was wrong. No, it was terrible.

His heart pounds and his calves burn. He stops running and begins to walk. Two pregnant women with racing numbers pinned to their chests pass him. He can't stop thinking. It's been all about wants: an impressive office, a fast car and an expensive house. Now, it's about what he needs: Deborah and the sound of her laughter, a look in her eye telling him to come home, a purpose in life besides making money. He'll finish the race only to talk to Alex and his family at the end. He will change even if it's too late.

He begins to jog. It doesn't matter if he wins. His breath is even. His body moves like it was built for this exact pace.

Twenty-Six

Tonight she plans to cook beef. It's still hot outside but the intensity of the summer has passed, the evenings are finally in the eighties.

Deborah sets the cloth bags down on the kitchen countertop. She unloads all the items into her refrigerator and reviews tonight's recipe in her head. She can't wait to present the meal and then a simple dessert. Maybe ice cream, she thinks. A small group from her photography class is coming over for dinner. There'll be five of them.

She's discovered that this new sense of life has fueled her appetite. Initially this surprised her. She'd thought that the shock of Amber tying her up and robbing her would have left her frozen and unable to eat. But clearly that wasn't the case. Instead it created a new desire.

She went to the local bookstore and bought cookbooks. She tried new recipes. At first she prepare gourmet meals for herself. Balsamic marinated beef tenderloin with herbs and dried tomato sauce. Sea bass poached in orange, basil and white wine with a citrus dressing. With the leftovers she'd make salads or sandwiches for lunch the following day.

Each week her love for cooking grew. After perfecting a recipe she'd invite new friends from her photography class to her condo for dinner. She enjoyed setting a table, preparing the meal and pouring a wine. There was laughter and stories to share about the past and present. She was surprised at how easily she was able to laugh at herself. She had future hopes.

They'd commiserate about the heat and the shared annoyance of out-of-town friends and family who all asked how they managed to survive the summer. As if escaping to a second home was an option for everyone. It certainly wasn't for her new group of friends. They all had jobs and responsibilities.

When her pants grew tighter she simply bought the next size up. As long as she exercised a few times a week and ate well she found that she didn't worry about her weight anymore. It was a relief to let that go. The days began to pass quickly. Soon it was the end of the summer.

Now she starts the meal so it will be ready in time. She thinks about what she'll make next weekend for Natalya's going away party. Natalya is moving to San Diego with a friend. Deborah is happy for her.

She takes out the tomatoes and carefully slices them on the plastic cutting board. She finishes and covers them with plastic. Next she removes the garlic, onion and basil. She begins with the onions. Immediately her eyes fill with tears. She wipes them away with the back of her hand but they continue. She smiles and continues her work.

Twenty-Seven

She'd only called about the car although Dan wasn't sure why. She didn't need his permission to sell it. Still, she said something about wanting to get the most value for it. "You'd have the type of friends who could afford it," she had said at one point in the conversation. Although he didn't admit it to her it stuck him as an insult. But sure enough, soon after the phone call, Brady Davidson piped up about needing a new car and within minutes the Range Rover was sold.

The next part that he didn't understand was why he volunteered to deliver it to Davidson in LA. But two days later, he finds himself in the company car being chauffeured to the desert. Dan leans back against the comfort of the reclining leather seats and closes his eyes. The driver attempts polite conversation while Dan feigns sleep.

He tells himself that he should enjoy the perks of this job while they're still available to him. He's turning in his letter of resignation at the end of this month. His plan is to take some time off and explore other opportunities. He's

tempted to leave Los Angeles altogether. He tries to imagine new possibilities. But he still feels a longing for Deborah. Soon he does fall asleep and when he opens his eyes
he finds himself at Deborah's condominium. He grabs his
briefcase, thanks the driver and tips him generously. He
stands and stretches. He watches the car turn out of the
parking lot and drive away.

Deborah's Range Rover is parked under an awning. It's
clean and still looks brand new. Davidson is getting a good
deal. He still can't believe that she's letting it go.

"I don't need a car like that here," she said during their
last phone conversation. "Besides, it's only me."

"What'll you get instead?" he asked.

"Something economical," she replied firmly.

Now he walks to her door. She even sounded different on the phone. He thought that the ordeal with Amber
handcuffing her to the bed would have rattled her. Instead
it seemed to have sparked a new strength and confidence.

He knocks on the door and she opens it. She even looks
different, he thinks. Her hair is wet, long and loose. She's
in her bathing suit with a towel wrapped around her hips.
They too have changed. Her girlish figure has become
womanly. He can't help but stare at her breasts. They look
full. She is beautiful, he thinks, but he dares not say it. He
doesn't want to risk being thrown out.

"Thanks for coming to pick it up," she says. She holds
the door open for him. Still, he stands on the threshold.
This is not his condo. "Come inside," she says, motioning
him forward. "You're letting out the air-conditioning."

He walks in. The place has been reorganized since
the robbery. Her photography lines the walls. The condo

looks nice. I could be comfortable here, he thinks. He feels ashamed at the memory of dismissing its value years ago. She had been right. It would have been a nice retreat from Los Angeles.

"Do you want a drink?" she asks and walks towards the kitchen. He can't help staring at her backside. Her skin is tanned and drops of water cling to her. "No thanks," he says. "I should go."

She turns and looks surprised. "I washed it this morning and filled it with gas," she says and picks up a set of keys from the kitchen counter. She walks them to him and places them in his open hand. "Thanks again," she says. Without warning she presses up against him and gives him a hug. The coolness of her wet bathing suit feels good. He puts his arms around her. He doesn't want to let go. She presses against him. He's afraid she feels his physical desire for her. As he starts to pull away she kisses him gently on the neck. He hadn't expected that. He pulls her closer. Then she turns her face upwards proffering a kiss. His mouth moves towards her. He can feel her breath. She smells like mints and chlorine. Had she wanted this before he came? It doesn't matter because now he kisses her. He couldn't stop himself. Gently but resolutely he presses his lips against hers. At first he shows the restrain of reluctance. Then she clutches him around his back with her cool wet arms. Her lips respond to his and the tip of her tongue brushes the inside of his mouth. He slides his hands along her smooth body. It could not happen, he tries to tell himself. He strains to prepare for the pain of rejection. But in moments they are kissing wildly. He slides her bathing suit straps down her arms. Soon her bathing suit and the towel drop to the floor. She stands naked before him and takes his hand. She leads him to her bedroom. He quickly unbuttons his tie and work shirt. His stomach is flat. She notices his good shape and reaches for him. He lies on top of her and she unzips his pants. His want for her is obvious.

"Are you sure about this, Deborah," he says.

She puts her hand over his mouth and crawls on top of him. Soon he is inside of her and they are moving and moaning in unison. When it's over he lies back unsure of what just happened. She stands and walks across the room. He watches her. "You're so beautiful," he says. He wants to say more but soon she is pulling on a robe. "Are you sure you don't want anything to drink?" she offers again casually, as though nothing has happened. She walks out of the room and closes the door behind her.

Dan lies there naked for a moment and suddenly feels foolish. He stands and picks his clothes off the floor. He gets dressed but leaves off his tie. He opens the bedroom door and finds her sitting at the small dining room table opening mail.

"Thanks again for helping me out with the whole car thing, Dan. I really do appreciate it," she says.

"You're welcome," he says unsure of how else to respond.

"Here are the keys," she says and stands. She walks them over to him and drops them in his hand with the tie. "You'd better start back to Malibu before traffic picks up," she says. She returns to her paperwork.

"Deborah, I don't know what to say," he says honestly.

"I think its best if you just go," she says and pretends to look busy.

He walks to the door opens it and steps outside. The sunlight is blinding. He looks back at her but she ignores him. He walks to the car. He hears her shut the door behind him but doesn't look back. He feels rejected.

He opens the car door and starts the engine. The car is filled with gas. Maybe I should go back, he thinks. But she seems so strong and clear about what she wants and what she doesn't. Reluctantly, he puts the car into reverse and then drives away.

Twenty-Eight

Toward the end of the fall Deborah turns on her new television and sees that Malibu is burning. The flickering light from the TV illuminates the room. She couldn't stop watching now even if she wanted to. She crosses her legs Indian-style on the couch. The fire started during the night and is approaching PCH. She wonders about Dan. It's almost noon on Saturday. He wouldn't be at work.

Deborah shoves a fistful of popcorn into her mouth and chews loudly. She believes that she has the sixth sense: she had the foresight to get out before all of this happened. She knew Malibu was a dangerous place. She watches as the fire envelops a beachfront home. "Get out as fast as you can," she'll say to lonely married women. She wipes her greasy fingers on her leggings. How far is the fire from their house? She watches in disbelief as firemen arrive from all over California. She stands and stretches her legs. The phone rings. She's happy to walk away from what she sees to answer it. She hopes maybe it'll be Dan.

"How is your house?" Natalya asks.

"I don't know yet," she answers.

"Have you heard from either of them?" Natalya asks.

Deborah knows she's referring to both Joe and Dan. It had felt good to talk about what she had left behind over the slow summer hours in the Date Shop.

"No, but the only one I'm worried about now is Dan," she says. "The other one seems to manage best on his own. I don't think of him at all these days." What she's said is true. He came to her sometimes during the first long days of summer in dreams. But now she finds that she feels upset with herself when she remembers him at all. His role in her life seems so obvious now. He'd served his purpose. "All the same, I do hope he's all right too," she says. She smiles when she imagines him out of danger, imagining that the expensive private Malibu rehab has paid for a private helicopter to airlift the addicts. She says goodbye and hangs up the phone.

The newscasters appear pleased with their story. "The Malibu Inferno," they call it. Deborah takes another handful of popcorn. Despite their best effort to look sympathetic they seem high from the excitement.

She calls the house and Dan's cell phone but can't get through. If the house burns down, she would like to watch it with him. After all, it was something they shared. No one else could understand what it had meant, for better or for worse. Her palms feel sweaty and she paces the small living room. She hasn't forgotten about the last time that he was here. Some days she finds herself physically longing for him.

She wonders how he spends his Saturdays. Her weekends are devoted to her photography project and visiting with new friends. Her teacher Vicki, an older woman with a long silver pony tail, has encouraged her work and offered to put Deborah in touch with a local gallery where she might be able to commission the series on desert animals. She'd like to share that good news with Dan. For the first time in years she finds herself really missing him. Despite the anger and disappointment there is a connection. She's not sure of what it is but it exists nonetheless. In a moment she decides what she must do.

Twenty-Nine

Of course she'd go back. Certainly not to stay but there's still work to be done. She won't leave things unfinished the way her mother had. Besides, it's what she owes not only to Dan but also to herself. So many times she walked away from what she thought would hurt her. But in the end, the pain never disappeared by her trying to ignore it. This is what she has learned.

She reads the sign, "Malibu, 27 miles of scenic beauty". She smiles knowingly. She is driving to make sure than Dan is safe and to see what's left of her house. She realizes that it had been hers too, even if she hadn't really wanted it. They'll face what is left of it together.

The ocean is sparkling. The sun is shining. It's a perfect day despite the smell of smoke and burned hillsides. The Malibu Inferno turned out to last a brief 24 hours but still engulfed her neighborhood and several beachfront homes.

I can't believe I lived here, she thinks. She signals and turns off PCH. The sides of the road up the canyon are covered in ashes. She wonders where Dan is staying. She drives toward her old street until she reaches a concrete barrier.

She parks her white compact car and grabs her camera from her trunk. Midway through the drive she had convinced herself that she was coming only to document what was left from the fire, but still she knew that she was looking for more. There were too many things left unsaid.

She climbs over the concrete roadblock, careful of her footing, climbing steadily and slowly up to her old house. The road will lead her back to where she came from. A journey. She follows the trail of collapsed chimneys until she reaches the one she recognizes as her own, not that it's easily distinguishable from the others now. A cemetery. The rehab is gone just like the other houses. There had been so much uproar because of it; it's just a pile of ash.

She raises her camera and steadies her hand before snapping the photographs that will be the inspiration for her next collection. Her house is destroyed. She shoots the broken and blackened remains of its concrete foundation. Despite the money and innovation that went into its planning and execution, this is all that remains. Destruction or rebirth? Deborah wonders.

Rebirth, she tells herself, aiming her lens at a blackened yucca tree still standing upon soot and sand. It's full of life and rising from the ashes. She keeps taking pictures. Like me, the yuccas are desert dwellers, she thinks. She takes photographs until she runs out of film.

The snapping sounds of dead branches behind her reminds her of the desert. She turns around. Dan looks good. Before she can stop herself she's smiling at him. He stands a few feet before her and looks at what remains of their house.

"I'm glad you're ok," she says.

"You are?" he asks. His clothes are covered in dirt. He had tried at first to stay and fight the flames with a garden hose. After a few minutes he realized that it wasn't worth the risk. After all, it was only a house. He retreated to the safety of a hotel in Santa Monica. He wants to tell her all of these things but doesn't know where to start.

"Yes, I worried about you for a change," she says.

He smiles. "Did you get some good pictures?" he asks, nodding at the camera hanging from her neck.

"We'll see. It's a process," she says looking down at the blackened earth, then up at him. "If you want I can show them to you when they're developed."

"I'd like that," he says. He thinks that if she gave him the chance, he'd enjoy watching her develop the film, but he doesn't want to ask for more. He wants to be content with the fact that she's willing to share this much of herself with him.

"What are you going to do now?" she asks.

He doesn't know if she's referring to the immediate or to the future. "For the first time in my life, I don't have a plan," he answers to either interpretation of her question.

Deborah studies him as if he's one of her subjects. His dark hair contrasts with his pale skin, just like hers. To an outsider, she realizes, they could look like relatives. They had spent more than a decade together, but it feels like she's seeing him for the first time.

A news van parks besides Deborah's car down the hill.

"Let's go," Deborah says. Maybe it's as easy as this.

They walk down what remains of the hill.

A heavily made up reporter carefully climbs the barrier and walks towards them. She's someone Deborah recognizes but can't name. All three of them stop in the middle of the road. The newscaster introduces herself and extends a manicured hand. "Did you lose your house?" she asks.

They nod.

"I'm sorry. That's awful, would you be willing to talk to me on camera?" she asks. She looks like she's searching their faces for traces of tears or expressions of hopelessness. But the woman will find neither.

Dan looks at Deborah. It's clear he wants some sign about how he should proceed but she doesn't offer him a clue. He shrugs. The newswoman looks at them impatiently.

Deborah thinks that the woman's high heels must be uncomfortable on this broken road.

"Actually, I'd rather be left alone to talk privately with her," he says gesturing toward Deborah, still unsure of how he wants to address her. Ex wife seems too cold. There's so much that he wants to confess and ask. All of the questions he's formulated in his mind while he was running. Things he should have discussed with her during their marriage. He has so many regrets.

The newswoman looks surprised but shrugs and walks away, and Dan and Deborah continue down towards the car. "I guess it's time for a change," Dan says. He steps over the roadblock and stops to offer her his hand.

"Change is already here," she says, taking it.

"You're right," he says. He has lost so many things but finds now that what matters most is Deborah.

"Do you want to talk about things over lunch?" she suggests.

"I'd like that," he says.

The news people are unloading equipment. A hawk circles overhead. And Deborah and Dan walk down the rest of the hill holding hands.